*No Lease on Life*

# No Lease on Life

## Lynne Tillman

Red Lemonade
Brooklyn, New York
2018

Library of Congress Cataloging-in-Publication Data

Tillman, Lynne.

No lease on life / by Lynne Tillman.
p .cm.
ISBN 978-1-935869-01-6
I. Title
PS3570.I42 N6 1998
813/.54—dc20
      92-17603


Cover design by Charles Orr
Interior design by Fogelson + Lubliner

Red Lemonade
Brooklyn, New York

*To Gary Indiana*

Be not forgetful to entertain strangers,
for thereby some have entertained angels unawares.
—Hebrews 13:2

Take anything, the land at your feet, and use it.
—William Carlos Williams

# Table of Contents

1    Introduction by Eileen Myles
9    Night and Day
105  Day and Night

Introduction *by Eileen Myles*

Suddenly we're all realizing that the nineties were twenty years ago. This cumulative feeling is not about math. It's more like a tiny feeling of awe at a passage of time just before that time actually became history. It's not nostalgia—that's for others. It's more like shock and then shock atomizes into details and that's what this book is made of. The exact sea of details by which you experience a time more than describe it. The list is a monster, a chimera, it wiggles. I tore a column out of the *New York Times* several months back anticipating writing this and in that column its author cried oh where is the contemporary novel of real estate, of rent. I thought buddy you should have been around twenty years ago. Cause what's happening now happened then. But better than saying that, read this. I had such a passion for Lynne Tillman's *No Lease On Life* when it came out in 1998. I could write about it at the drop of a hat and I did. I wrote about it several times and here I am writing again. Because . . . well, you know how you have certain stories in your life made of details that are so etched onto your chakras that you could tell that story on a boat in the middle of a storm if you had to. And I suppose that storm is memory. There are books that other people write for you that kindle that same sensation in the *I wish I said that* way. Lynne Tillman made the particular suffering and humor that we lived in and called a neighborhood (and a sensibility) in the East Village of the seventies, eighties, ending in the nineties be just as intelligent and precise and as sleepless and angsty and certain of its own moral rectitude as it could possibly be without ever for a moment abandoning its own essential hopelessness. This is such funny lonely work. The narrator's a chorus of one consumed with a sense that everything keeping her up (on her wire of sleepless thinking) is both terribly wrong and precisely hers somehow. There's things she plans to do in response but I don't want to ruin the book. I want the book to ruin you! Plus none of that is the point. What's most amazing to me about this work today is that she needed to perform her own *rendition*. In *all* the meanings of the word. Her book is prophetic. Her recital of the nineties is like a micro testing "it" out. Lynne was palping the world. The one we were already living in. Consciously or not she was gauging the immediate effects of certain public decisions. Deregulation. The abandonment of an entire generation of veterans. Ending of overtime wages under Bush. Opening of mental hospitals, letting the patients just figure it out. Believe me it was no king of hearts.

I remember the very upper middle class husband of a friend of my then girlfriend, saying smilingly at dinner one night in the late nineties (almost the end) that Giuliani had taken the city back. For who?

I guess he was right but first they let it get worse. What would that be like. A relentless poem like Lynne's: a Kandor—a tiny model of what would also be inflicted on suspected terrorists and soon the whole rest of the world that by now is being returned home. Or maybe it was returned home to us first. Dropped on everyone but the very rich. The bottom for a time went so much lower, the homeless and there were so many of them were shitting in the subway because deregulation meant that there were no bounds to the amount of suffering that could now be exposed in our test case neighborhood that later on got "fixed." And it worked. Everyone still wonders where they—the poor, the homeless, the junkies went. I think of this book as a long song. Cause there's no plot and it's a novel of that. It's just exposed pain. The pain around her and the pain inside her. A neighborhood howling out loud. Naturally there were bands. They let us have that. It's the end of the early phase of an ongoing political situation. A woman lives in a building with her boyfriend (a musician) and she's from a middle class background, maybe upper middle class even suburban and the building she lives in is maintained by a completely dysfunctional super. And her landlady, a monster, doesn't care. And the super in the building across the way works on his car and runs its motor in the wee hours of the morning. And there's a gang she calls the morons who laugh and punch each other and throw trash barrels around all night. And she can't stop them. There is so much she is helpless about in this book and so the book itself may be a little bit or a lot like *Bleak House* is occurring so much in her mind. It's a long complaint recalling all of her life in this city and the various men she's slept with (and the good one beside her now) and the unimportant job she holds at the time of the telling of the book. And you think it's just that in its pure excess, in its detailed high contrast black and white inky drawing of mental anguish and pain because she cannot sleep she cannot ever sleep but finally something else really marvelous occurs in this book. Jokes. I suppose I think it's a massively Jewish book because of the jokes. The jokes bleed right out of the mental pain of the narrator. She's good at complaining. It's a vaudeville neighborhood. She comes from a culture of complaint. And these are really some of the funniest jokes I've ever read. Do you have a joke-book. Have you ever owned a book of jokes in your life. Maybe when you were a kid.

When I reread this book the jokes seemed even funnier now and I felt compelled to try them out in social situations. And every time a joke changes "it" up. It's the bomb. Because once it's been demonstrated to you that whole city is conspiring to keep you awake and no one, not the city, not your lover, not your super or your peers no drug can relieve you of this pain then something made of the very same substance like Kryptonite or a vaccine is the only cure. Because is it the noise out there well sure certainly the pain, the hell is a world in which people do shit and piss and have sex in your doorway and block your door with their bodies because they have shot drugs in your hall because the door between your hallway and the world is never locked and your super won't fix it and your landlady doesn't care so anyone can come and take a crap or shoot their drugs probably leaving their needles behind. So something that copies all that—your very own mind creates a relay so that you can't even imagine any way out of it or it ever changing but somehow you must subvert this second monstrosity, your rendition, and a joke does just that. It interrupts hell by creating almost a koan. It's like the day that was so bad that the only ease is thinking how much worse it can get and making a little bright suitcase full of the kind of pain that anyone could understand. Someone walks onto the set of a film of the absolute worst day in your life and they are a cartoon character and they walk onto that movie set and leave a little suitcase and it is a bomb and everybody blows up and then the story goes on relieved somehow. Is it how women are different. They don't simply go out and kill people I mean in a regular way like in history, mostly women don't make war. They just bleed once a month. And maybe that sight makes us a little different about the positive effects of war on a culture or violence in a family. She probably doesn't come home from work and smack her husband around. Or her wife. Well this is a heterosexual story so I'll keep it like that. And the morons up all night throwing the trash cans around are mostly men. The ridiculous female characters here are like her sometime neighbor who does tricks on the corner in her own neighborhood where she grew up. But that's not the same as keeping people up with noise or violence is it. In a way the woman who sells sex is making a joke about the woman who thinks she doesn't. To interrupt a never ending saga, say patriarchy, or expanding capitalism with a sad vaudeville act where someone marches out into their own little square just when you forgot that this happens and sings a little song, tells a joke, an offbeat version of the trashcans banging but it's orderly somehow, and you go ok I'll bite, knock knock. Who's there. I can't sleep anyway. And because they—the people who say things are now saying that black holes aren't singularities, dense ends of matter that simply kill, that simply crush with gravitational force. That just as the darkness squeezes almost tighter than you can bear, just when not being able to sleep almost produces an aneurysm you are straining so hard in your head something opens instead and the voyager flies through to another universe, a parallel one perhaps you land lightly in a doorway that resembles yours but for briefly or was it a thousand years who knows about time in the respite of a laugh the old welcome rug with the condom on it looks almost beatifically great and strange. You kick it to the side and step in. Lynne Tillman's singular novel reminds me of a city that almost broke and while speeding to the bottom you were accompanied by an enormously compassionate, righteously angry, particular and venomously interesting heart so you could always tap your way through and I would give this book to anyone I loved and tell them that this is how we lived in the city.

---

Eileen Myles is a poet, novelist, performer and art journalist. Their twenty books include *Afterglow (A Dog Memoir)*, *I Must Be Living Twice: New and Selected Poems*, a 2017 re-issue of *Cool for You* and *Chelsea Girls*.

Night and Day

Clip, clop, clip, clop—BANG.
Clip, clop, clip, clop—BANG BANG.
Clip, clop, clip, clop—BANG.
Clip, clop, clip, clop—BANG BANG.
What's that?
I don't know.
An Amish drive-by shooting.

They were just fucking around. They yelled and ran. They overturned all the garbage cans on her block. They were probably going to the park. They were methodical. They turned them over, one after another, and bellowed. They leaped around, up and down, and then one of them—four males and a female—threw a garbage can at a first-floor window. He missed. Then he and another guy aimed garbage cans at a car, which they hit. Any moron can hit a car with a garbage can.

Car alarms went off. No one could sleep. Windows opened wide. People hung out their windows. Their mouths hung open too. It was pathetic.

Elizabeth was looking out her window.

Everyone was asleep and in messed-up T-shirts or ratty robes, tied strangely at the waist. They all looked strangled. It was the middle of the night or the morning. It was hot. Only people with their air conditioners on ever slept through the night. That's how the block divided in the summer, with A/C or without. It was pathetic.

Elizabeth wanted to kill them. Someone should kill them. She wanted to use a crossbow and steel arrow. Much easier to buy than a gun, entirely legal, no waiting period. But crossbows had just been on the news, and she suspected that everyone would be buying them, the way everyone suddenly bought red eyeglasses. Maybe she was too exhausted to be unique, but she would take severe satisfaction in shooting an arrow right into a guy's head—right through the middle of it, between his eyes or from one ear to the other. He'd look like a comic book character sporting that goofy toy parents bought for their kids years ago. Made them look like they'd had their skulls split in half.

Elizabeth's arrow would be real, and she'd murder the guy, and the instant before his death, he'd be surprised, but still he'd exhibit no remorse and she'd feel no regret. The cops would be called. She'd be taken away. So what if she went to jail. She'd have the support of the neighborhood, the block anyway. She didn't have a record. How long would they keep her in. Eight years was the max. She wasn't sure why, but that figure occurred to her. Maybe because she'd heard about a serial rapist who'd been let out after eight years and he'd mutilated one of his victims, left her to die. That's cruel. Maybe she'd be able to read in jail. She wondered if it was quiet in there. She wondered if the women were as noisy as the men or noisier or not noisy at all. There have been so few women in prison movies, she didn't know. She'd kill a white guy. Maybe he'd even be in school or have a job, so his weekend, late-night marauding would be less likely to be described as driven or desperate. Her victim would be no deprived social misfit. Just a jerk, a prankster. She wasn't Bernhard Goetz, subway vigilante, going berserk and into overkill.

She'd kill someone like herself, she'd make a clean hit, have a clean and lucid, if angry, response. It would be a reaction, and, she'd be called a reactionary. She could handle that, especially in jail, where other people would've done much worse things. More senseless anyway. Her reaction would be considered crazy, or she would be. Everyone she knew would think she was nuts and had overreacted. She could hear people saying that, see their mouths moving, and she felt like throwing up.

Everyone would know what it was about. She'd make sure of that. It was about being able to sleep through the night. Being able to turn down your covers and get into bed and not have to wake every hour and run to the window because someone was screaming, sitting on a stoop, screaming and laughing or blasting music and yelling. About nothing. It was always stupid stuff. But even if it was smart, she'd hate it, hate them. Who cares then.

She couldn't sleep. She might as well stand by the window, vigilant about nothing. 911 didn't come unless you screamed Murder.

Some neighborhood morons who lived on the street, not bridge and tunnel or whatever, woke her the other night. They were on the church steps, playing stickball with glass bottles. Yelling every time a bottle shattered. It was 5 A.M. Elizabeth opened the window as wide as it would go, and stuck her head and body out. She watched one of the males saunter to the pile of beer bottles and choose one carefully. As if it mattered what kind of bottle he hit. Three females followed the play like despondent cheerleaders. Another male wound up, on the street mound, and pitched to the hitter. He missed. The bottle shattered. The hitter assumed the stance for another swing.

Elizabeth restrained herself from leaping onto the fire escape.

She walked through the dark apartment, trying not to wake Roy. She phoned the precinct. The desk cop said he'd send a car. Thirty minutes passed. They were still shrieking. Bottles crashed to the ground again end again Elizabeth called the precinct again. The precinct's phone machine answered. At the end of the recorded message, the same cop picked up:

—Fifth Precinct.

—This is the woman who called before.

—Yeah.

—There's been no car.

—Yeah? You haven't seen it? Cause I sent one.

—I haven't seen it. and I've been standing here pretty much for the whole thirty minutes.

—Yeah. . . . Well. I sent one.

—They're still breaking bottles. I can't sleep.

—Yeah. I asked for a car, but we're a little busy this time of night. . . . Unfortunately.

Unfortunately. The cop sounded rueful. It was rueful. Having to call cops or be a cop. At least he hadn't lied. She hated being lied to. Except that she lied too. When Elizabeth phoned about an all-night party, a female cop said, We're sending a car. The car never came, the music kept blasting. Elizabeth took a pill. The party was for the Policemen's Benevolent Association. In the basement of the church where a variety of morons often sat on the steps.

Now Elizabeth leaned out the window. Garbage was everywhere. She'd murder the guy. She'd murder him with an acute pleasure that might last only a second. It would thrill wildly in her body for an evanescent, unimportant moment, but it might be worth it. He was bouncing up and down now, rocking with laughter at how the car's window had shattered, how broken bottles were lying everywhere, how spilled garbage wantonly littered the sidewalk. It would rot and become fetid. It would rot and smell. She was rotting and rotten. She would smell when it came time for her to die.

The arrow would pierce his insignificant, preemie brain, and blood would spurt from the wound, the way it did in a Peckinpah movie, which is the only thing you remember about his movies, so it was a mistake to do it, not what she was intending, what Peckinpah did. A special effect is no legacy. She'd say her response was about— she'd say this when she was interviewed—not hatred, but dignity and a social space, a civil space, actually a civilian space. Not a place where life is a series of unwanted incidents. A place where people could thrive without having to move to the country or a small city, to expire quietly from lack of interest. She'd wax romantic about what you could expect or hoped to get from other people, and what you didn't get. She'd call it respect. Everyone did.

You talk mostly about what you're not getting. Respect, sex, money, sleep. If you have it, you don't need to mention it. When you have it, you're bored if other people even bring it up. Of course, people with lots of money also think about it all the time and want more of it, were afraid of losing it, but they probably had the sense not to talk about wanting it in public.

The morons were spilling garbage on the church steps. They were proud. The wild ones, the wild morons. The mild ones. Roy called himself and his friend Joe the mild ones. Elizabeth laughed silently.

She was capable of doing it, she could murder them. She didn't care. In prison she'd laugh maniacally, she'd sing, she'd write her jail notes, she'd take care of birds, she'd become famous for her legal acumen, she'd find a calling, she'd discover the nobility of suffering. She'd destroy herself meticulously.

The morons were proud of how they destroyed things. Things are easily destroyed. Elizabeth was proud of her restraint. She didn't climb out the window and run down the fire escape, holding her robe so her nakedness wouldn't be exposed, fly onto the street, arms flailing, and strangle them or stab them repeatedly, leaving a multitude of gashes. They wouldn't know what hit them.

She might lose her mind, lose herself, just long enough to be declared legally incompetent, temporarily insane, and do it.

Judge, your honor, I found myself standing on the street in my robe and my hands were around his neck. Their necks. I had a knife in my hand. I don't know who put it there. I was surrounded by dead people. They were everywhere. Blood was everywhere. It was awful. I don't know what happened. There was so much noise and then I saw red. I suppose it was blood. And everything went black. I fainted dead away.

She probably wouldn't say fainted dead away.

The fantasy contented her for a vacant minute. It became the content of her life. Her fantasies were tacky home movies, not features. At the movies she wasn't in her own world, she was in another world that was hers for the time of the movie. Ninety minutes, two hours, three hours. In her own movie house, she was wrapped up, projecting, and it might just be a few seconds. A few seconds devours a lifetime.

Time was getting later or earlier. Elizabeth had spots in front of her eyes. The clock rested on a black metal stool. It turned time out and over. Like garbage. Elizabeth—the Lizard, to Roy—stared at its eternally dumb face. She watched the little hand spit its way forward. The hands of time jerked on. How much time would it take to murder the morons. She clenched her hands. They weren't big enough to strangle anyone big.

A couple strolled on the other side of the street. They were holding hands, their arms and bodies entangled, octopus like, they were devouring each other. Then they saw the garbage. They moved away fast into the middle of the empty street. They kissed there. There were no cars around. Just garbage. And rats. The lovers didn't care about the rats underground or behind the garbage cans, their homes uprooted. Love lets you forget rats. She wondered which of them would be disappointed first. Which of the lovers. The disappointment of rats was beyond her.

When she and Roy were new, sometimes she waited for him to come home. She'd stare at the clock's face, expecting it to talk. The hands ticked, Where is he? Then he'd show up, tock, tick, drunk, impish, surly, or tired. She'd be angry, ragged, or relieved. With time passing, that didn't happen anymore. She didn't worry when he came in. She trusted Roy. He had no reason to hurt her. Not that you had to have a reason to hurt somebody.

Roy was sleeping.

He was inexplicable. They loved each other, whatever that was. Sometimes they hated each other. They had love scenes and hate scenes. They interested each other over time. He wished Elizabeth cooked, but she didn't.

Lights turned on across the street. Third floor. A man leaned out. T-shirt, no shorts, no pants. Hard to tell. He was half a body. He stared down at the garbage and then across and up. He looked her way, like TV screens registering each other. Elizabeth moved away, to the side of the window, so that she couldn't be seen, only in profile, if at all. She couldn't really tell if he was looking at her. If he was, she couldn't tell if his look was complicitous, a garbage-thrower-watching look, or hostile, lascivious, or sinister. She couldn't tell if he was a danger to her or the community. At a distance it's hard to tell who's an enemy. She wouldn't be able to identify him in a lineup. The distance was too great. His face was mushy, blurred. She couldn't make him, she'd tell the cop who was encouraging her to nail the guy. She couldn't say, Yes, that's him, instead she'd have to say, I can't make a positive identification. The cop would be pissed and tell the other officers out of earshot, except she'd hear, She couldn't ID the guy. Scared.

The man in the third-floor window turned his light off.

Elizabeth didn't know if he was a potential enemy. She had some enemies. A couple had been friends of hers. It's hard to make a positive ID even when you're up close. Her best friend had been the worst. Her mother hated Elizabeth. Elizabeth was a threat. She remembered that and her friend's big, placid, lying eyes, her laugh, and that her friend hated to vomit. Now, whenever Elizabeth thought about her, she thought about vomit. Another friend schemed behind her back. Elizabeth found out. The friend manipulated everyone. She had no friends. She didn't know that.

A few enemies were strays, accidental acquaintances. Accidents are sometimes dressed up as people. She'd had sex with some accidents. Accidents were always waiting to happen. Maybe she'd looked at someone funny once. Maybe she'd sided with someone in an unimportant bar argument and another person she hadn't even noticed became enraged. This person was plotting against her secretly. She had a few secret enemies.

A couple of her enemies were blatant. They were disappointed, dangerously overweight men. She worked with them one week on, one week off, in the proofroom. She read proof with them. It was an outdated occupation. The two fat men taught her not to sympathize automatically with unhappy people. The emotionally crippled and downtrodden can be vicious. She worked with a lot of miserable people. There were many miserable people in the company, misery wants company. Proofreading didn't make her miserable. She liked focusing on typos and misspellings, on periods, commas, quotation marks, neutral characters in her life.

Five out of ten working days she rolled out of bed and over to the proofroom and worked late into the night. Ten hours, twelve hours, silver time, golden time, good overtime. The first time she saw the proofroom, she was in the building to take a proofreading test. She'd prepared and memorized the symbols, for delete, add, cap, small cap, wrong font. They were listed in any adequate dictionary.

Elizabeth didn't know it, but on the way to the test, she passed her future co-workers. They were sitting in a small room, with no door, at a long table, reading aloud to each other. Doing hot reads, she learned after she had the job. When you read silently to yourself, it's a cold read. It was confusing, six voices going simultaneously, people reading business articles to each other. Others were eating take-out food from different restaurants, but all the restaurants used the same plastic or Styrofoam containers. Some were reading the paper. Some were waiting for copy to come through a slot in the wall.

There's a field of ostriches. They all have their heads stuck in the ground. Another ostrich comes along. He looks around and says, Hey, where is everybody?

The proofreaders were low down in the company. It was obvious from their exposed quarters. The proofroom was similar to a stall in a barn, there was no privacy. No door, no windows. Company status was exhibited by the size of the office, the number of windows, closeness to the boss, a door that shuts others out. Status used to be access to the telephone, but now even janitors in the company had remotes.

The proofroom had one phone for twelve people. Even though proofreaders might do nothing for hours, might be waiting for the editors to edit, for the writers to finish writing or the fact checkers to check facts, they weren't supposed to be in touch with the outside world.

During their work time they were supposed to be available. They were supposed to be ready for copy that dropped through a slot in the wall like slop thrown at pigs or food shoved under the door for prisoners in isolation. When the pages would finally drop through the slot into the metal basket, they produced a swishing sound. All the proofreaders would hear it. The person nearest the slot in the wall was the supervisor or the next in command. One of them took the copy out of the basket, logged it in, and handed it out.

The proofreaders were a despised minority, a rung above the lowest group, the mailroom workers. The mailroom was in the basement. The mailroom workers were male, mostly black or Hispanic. Occasionally, when Elizabeth mailed one of her own letters and didn't want it routed through the system, because she wasn't supposed to use the company's system, she hand-delivered it to the mailroom. She went down in the elevator. She saw the black and Hispanic men. They were always surprised when one of the people from above came down. They stopped sorting the mail briefly to take in her presence, or anyone's. Though she was a nothing in the company's eyes, she still came from the world above, two floors up. It was pathetic.

The proofreaders were white, college graduates, middle-class misfits who accepted inferior jobs and were not ambitious. They had no future except the copy desk. The copy desk was allowed to change sentences. Proofreaders could only correct mistakes in spelling or find errors in fact. Any other change had to be reported to the desk. The proofreaders were beneath the desk, beneath contempt. The proofreaders were also beneath the janitors, who called the head of the company Boss. The janitors lived in houses in the suburbs and had two cars.

Elizabeth had won the steady part-time job over many applicants. She'd scored high on the test and the head of the room liked her best. Elizabeth had worn black socks with heels, a black jacket, and black pants to her interview. The socks made her a weirdo in the supervisor's eyes. The supervisor decided she'd fit in with the room. The proofreaders referred to their quarters as "the room." It was a correctional facility, Roy said.

A doctor said to his patient: I've got some good news and some bad news. The bad news is that you have two weeks left to live. The good news is that I fucked my secretary this morning.

Elizabeth joined the proofroom with reluctance. She was getting older, freelance didn't cut it anymore, and the room provided health insurance. If she was hit by a car or contracted HIV or MS, she was covered. The company also had a pension plan.

The room didn't let outside light in, it kept them separated from the world. While Elizabeth did hot reads and cold reads, even while she focused on the little black marks on shiny white paper, she deliberately thought about other things. She tested herself. It was possible to catch mistakes without being resigned. She never entirely submitted to the page at hand.

Elizabeth liked some of her fellow workers. Even one of the disappointed fat men had his moments. Everyone does. The other disappointed fat man was her sole implacable foe. He was unattractive and self-righteous. He collected stamps. He was easy to hate, and he hated her. He despised her. She could see it in his eyes. He was a company boy. Every time Elizabeth used the company mail he was offended, outraged. She flaunted it in front of him whenever she could. She liked having him as an enemy.

—Enemies last longer than friends, enemies define you, friends don't, Elizabeth said to Roy.

—They're both under dickheads in the dictionary.

—Dickheads won't be in there.

Apart from her enemies who had been her friends, and apart from some of her co-workers who hated her, Elizabeth had pretty good relations with friends and with most people on the block.

Except her landlord's manager, Gloria. Elizabeth complained to Gloria about the upkeep of the building. There was no upkeep. Gloria was married to the owner. She had a vested interest.

Elizabeth modulated her voice when she complained to Gloria. The Big G always smiled. It was a careful, broad smile. It was plastered across a too-rouged white face. Elizabeth would let them know when there was a gas leak, if there was the sick smell of gas in the building. She'd tell them there was no heat or hot water that day. Gloria always thanked her. Gloria was blustery and bad-tempered. She enjoyed deceiving tenants, renting and not renting, evicting or threatening eviction, delaying work on broken-down apartments, stalling tenants about the boiler in the basement being fixed or replaced.

Elizabeth didn't want to linger next to Gloria in the office. The Big G reeked of discontent, of frustration. From Gloria's point of view, she was made to sweat unnecessarily. She was the one who was wronged. When the Big G spoke about how hard it was being a landlord, how many things they had to take care of, how many boilers were broken down and how many tenants in their buildings didn't have heat and hot water, she rustled with indignation.

We don't have the time to get to the halls. But, dear, we'll get to it as soon as we do. We have emergencies right now. I'll talk to Hector when I have the chance.

Hector was the super of the building. Hector lived on the first floor. He'd been the super way before Elizabeth and Roy moved in. He was entrenched. Hector was a courtly man, part French, Greek, and Spanish. Talking to him about cleaning the halls, which was his job, was like talking to the morons on the street, Hector was imperious to dirt. He was completely unmoved by and indifferent to dirt and emergencies. He caused dirt and emergencies.

What Elizabeth wanted was modest. Relatively clean halls and stairs.

Elizabeth tried to reason with Gloria.

—Our halls need to be cleaned weekly.

—The people in apartment F, they're the problem. It's their cigarettes. They're pigs.

—It's not just them. The halls get dirty. They need to be cleaned weekly.

—The super's too old.

—Why don't you hire someone to help Hector, once a week for twenty-five dollars?

—We can't afford that.

—We shouldn't have to live with garbage in the halls.

—Hector has a drinking problem.

—I know.

—You get rid of Hector. Get a petition going with the other tenants.

—I don't want to get rid of Hector. Your job is to keep the building clean.

The Big G clenched her teeth.

—Do you know Hector hates you? she said.

—What?

—Hector hates you.

—Why are you telling me this?

—I think you should know.

—Why do I need to know?

—I think you should know.

—Have you told Hector I'm the one complaining about the halls?

—You must have complained to him.

—I haven't talked to him, except to say hello, in two years. You
told him I was complaining.

The Big G was trapped in a discoverable lie. People lie about
the obvious. People do the obvious. Elizabeth lifted her head
high and told the Big G she was cruel. Then she walked out of the
office. Hector's alcoholism and indifference to filth, and the Big G's
obnoxious presence, were preferable to nothing, to no super at all.
For a long time Elizabeth avoided the Big G and hardly ever called the
office. If she saw Gloria on the street, Elizabeth pretended to be blind.

She was no more blind than most people. Elizabeth noticed
other buildings in the neighborhood. Some of their halls gleamed.
They shocked her with their simple cleanliness, which was just an
absence of filth. Her friend Larry's building was clean. He paid less
rent than she did. He liked her apartment better. It was bigger. Maybe
her friend Larry's hallways were clean because he had a super who
was like her aunt and uncle. They cleaned their apartment the whole
weekend, together. They enjoyed it. After she found out what they
did every weekend, Elizabeth stopped visiting them.

Maybe, Elizabeth decided, the point was to hire someone
who's compulsive about dirt, someone who has to clean. Someone
who'd be happy to do it for nothing. Some halls and buildings
were immaculate. She'd seen them. Some garbage cans were not
overflowing. Some buildings had enough garbage cans, and garbage
wasn't all over the street. If they had someone who was obsessed
with dirt, who was driven to be clean, someone you wouldn't want
to know, but someone who was essentially harmless, and they hired
him or her to help Hector, life would be better.

Roy told Elizabeth she was crazy.

A man goes to Hell and the Devil says, I usually don't do this, but I'll give you your choice of room for eternity. So he takes the man to the first room. All the people are ankle deep in shit. In the second room all the people are knee-deep in shit. In the third room all the people are waist-deep in shit, and they're drinking coffee. The man says, I guess I'll take the third room. The Devil says, OK. Then he turns to the people in the third room and yells, Coffee break's over. Back on your heads.

Elizabeth knew the halls could be maintained, even in her degraded neighborhood. It couldn't be accomplished if the super, whose job was to clean and maintain the building, was a pathological junk collector.

Hector was incapable of throwing anything out. He was attached to garbage. He was like a vampire running a blood bank or a pyromaniac firefighter. The firefighter goes rushing to a fire, he knows what his job is, to put out the fire, but he's on the fire-red engine, where he's wanted to be ever since his mouth was snatched away from his mother's breast, and now he's racing to a fire, he's along for the ride, for the thrill of it, and once he's there, he doesn't want to extinguish the fire. The flames shoot up around him, they engulf him like a large woman, he's swallowed up and warm. But he looks around, and he sees his buddies in danger, and they see him. He's hanging back, or worse, he's feeding the flames, so he has to pretend to fight the fire he loves. If there aren't enough fires, he sets them. He's unfit for his job.

Hector the super.

Sol Wachtler was chief justice of New York State. He stalked and threatened a woman who'd rejected him. You'd think that a judge who jails people for committing stupid, venal acts, who get caught by making asinine mistakes, would not make them himself. He can't stop himself, can't help himself. He's possessed, obsessed. Wachtler threatens her—her name is Joy—over his car phone. Traceable. Stupid.

Hector the super and Gloria.

There was a Mets catcher, Mackey Sasser. He had to quit playing. He developed a block against throwing the ball back to the pitcher on the mound. He couldn't throw it. He could throw the ball over the pitcher's head, to the second baseman, but not to the pitcher. The Mets put him in the outfield for a while. It wasn't his position. His position was behind the batter, squatting. But he was neurotic, blocked. His time in baseball was over.

Hector the super was blocked. He couldn't do the job he was paid to do.

Hector's apartment was incomprehensible. He, his wife, their grown children and their kids and an old dog lived in it. It was like the halls and stairs. But it was also cluttered with old newspapers, boxes, broken knickknacks, unrepairable lamps, and bottles for recycling that were never recycled, only stored. The overwrought apartment was stacked with unusable junk from the street. Sometimes, when Elizabeth happened to be walking downstairs or upstairs, and Hector or his wife happened to open their door a crack, she spied a narrow pathway between piles of boxes. She saw years of accumulation, things hanging from the ceiling and everything thrown together, piled up, even several broken-down wooden dressers stacked on top

27

of each other that reached to the ceiling. She couldn't take it in. The halls and marble stairs in a turn-of-the-century building built for immigrant labor could be kept tidy, even though the building stood shabby and tired in a mongrel neighborhood. It couldn't if the super's attitude toward his own apartment challenged and expanded the limits of what was fit for human habitation. His apartment exceeded standards. It was a mental condition, an excessive response to the burden of the physical world on the mental one. There didn't seem to be a table or chairs. There didn't seem to be chairs to sit on or beds, but she couldn't see that far back into the long apartment.

They probably ordered out. She and Roy ordered take-out from Chinese, Thai, and Italian restaurants. On another night Elizabeth was walking along the street. A foreigner approached her.

—Please, could you ask me, he said.

—Tell you.

—What means no menus?

Buildings have NO MENUS signs in their windows or on their front doors. Thousands of menus for take-out restaurants are thrown into vestibules. It's the super's job to get rid of them. Hector never did. He didn't even save them. Elizabeth picked them up and threw them out. The Big G said it wouldn't pay to put a notice in the window saying NO MENUS. Restaurants ignored them.

—No menus means the tenants of the building don't want restaurants to advertise their menus for take-out food. . .

—Take-out food?

—Take-out food is food you can order over the phone from a restaurant. The restaurant delivers it to your apartment.

—Delivers?

—They send a boy or a man on a bicycle usually. He carries the food you ordered.

—Why take out?

—So you don't have to cook. So that you don't have to go out to eat. You can eat in.

—Eat in?

—Eat in your apartment. It's short for eat in your apartment.

—No menus, thank you, he said.

—You're welcome, Elizabeth said.

He turned away. He appeared confused. He looked at the sign on the door again. NO MENUS. He was apartment hunting. He turned her way again. He pointed to the sign and, after an exaggerated sigh of relief, mimed for her benefit, he smiled poignantly. He waved good-bye.

Because of Hector, the landlord regularly received health and building violations. The landlord had to pay the City for the misdeeds of its super. Finally Hector was ordered by the City to clean out the basement. It was a fire hazard.

Modern architects denied buildings basements and attics, banished them. Basements were where people had stored the inadmissible and unnecessary. The modern idea was rational, no one should hold on to anything, people should live neatly in a clean place in the present, which was ridiculous, since the present is collecting irrationally as the past, but now, with those disorderly shelters gone, everyone had to get rid of things continuously. There was no breathing room for the wretched, the worthless, the disgusting, the disreputable.

Sometimes Elizabeth understood Hector.

The basement in this premodern tenement was like his

apartment, but it was home to the boiler. Hector's behavior and activity in the irrational basement was an immediate, imminent fire hazard. Oil, rags, and newspapers were stored near the boiler. He left them to combust.

Hector stored junk in the hallway. No one could get past his door. You had to shove cartons out of your way. Your clothes got dirty. There was no path. There'd be no chance in a fire. A News Channel 4 Special reported that a fire engulfs a tenement in seconds, no one gets out alive. Everyone in her building would die, no tenant had a chance to escape, because Hector's crap was blocking the exit. There were fire escapes. But if you weren't near them, the front door was the rational exit. There was no rational exit. She didn't want to be burned to death.

Hector couldn't contain it, himself. He couldn't stop it, himself. He couldn't control himself or what he'd collected. It spread everywhere. The landlord didn't fire him. The Big G said it was because they were trying to help him. Hector was old, he was an alcoholic, he had worked for them a long time, he was nice. Everyone felt sorry for him. No one wanted him to lose his job. He was just in the wrong job. But they didn't fire him mostly because Hector worked cheap. He added to his puny salary by collecting bottles, the ones he hardly ever returned. He couldn't give them in.

In the spring, summer, and fall, Hector and his wife set up a table in front of the building to sell some of the stuff he found on the street, couldn't keep, or couldn't throw out. Elizabeth despaired of the table in front of the building. Elizabeth discarded shoes or clothes in garbage bags. She set them on the sidewalk. Her throwaways landed on the table outside the building. She'd see a pair of her torn underpants or a ripped sweater hours later. Homeless people had no chance to rummage through the garbage bags and find something to wear. Even if she no longer owned it, after throwing it away, she was frustrated to see it lying forlorn on Hector's table. Mrs. Hector usually sat behind the table, grinning. In the heat of summer, Mrs. Hector relaxed under an umbrella. She watched TV too. They had an extension cord that ran from their apartment to the street.

No one on the street could have anything for nothing. Even the most useless object. It happened everywhere, shoplifted books, furniture off the back of a truck, the worn and the used, peoples' lives on the ground, bargains on blankets.

Everyone wanted a bargain. Even if it was stolen.

There was a man on Eighth Street and Sixth Avenue at Christmas selling answering machines in their boxes for twenty dollars. Elizabeth was with her friend Helen. The guy hawked hard and fast. A crowd gathered around him.

—With a remote, twenty dollars. A bargain.

—Can I see one?

—Factory sealed.

The hawker held up a box.

—Why's a piece of tape there? It was opened.

—Factory rejects, lady, you want it or you don't. Twenty dollars.
    A bargain. Remote.

All the while he's talking to her, he's selling them briskly to people rushing by, people listening for thirty seconds, people convinced quickly. They take twenties out of their bags or pockets, then move on. A bargain. Elizabeth wanted a new answering machine. She hesitated. Helen said, If you want it, get it. Elizabeth handed the hawker a twenty, took the answering machine. She and Helen went for coffee. Elizabeth opened the box and pulled out a brick.

That was a while ago.

It was weird to see your torn underpants, your former underpants, with a fifty cents sign pinned to them. Elizabeth would glance at the table, her rejects, and smile at Hector's wife.

Mrs. Hector was friendly. The Hectors were good people. Mrs. Hector always said hello. She lifted her head up and down. She patted the dog. Their dog was big and slow, an old dog with a human name. Elizabeth would shake her head up and down in return or say hello. Then she'd go upstairs. She'd go inside. Elizabeth had no place inside for Mrs. Hector's table outside, though it was there. She didn't mention it to anyone.

—He's the one who's supposed to keep the halls clean, Roy.

—Drop it.

—It's insane.

—So what.

—Why do we have to live like this?

—Forget it.

Sometimes Elizabeth had the urge to sneak in and view Hector's apartment, the way she viewed dead bodies in coffins at funerals. From a distance, tentatively.

Now Frankie walked out to the street. He usually opened up the laundromat. That's strange, Elizabeth thought, staring at Frankie, who didn't notice her at the window, at least she didn't think he did, because if he did, he would say Hey or yo, they went back years together, it was too early for the laundromat to open. Frankie probably couldn't sleep either.

Elizabeth's chin rested on her hand. The night air was becoming lighter and thinner, distended.

Frankie lived in the Lopez apartment two floors below Roy and her. His mother had died not long ago. Elizabeth had known Frankie since he was five. Now he was an adult, he played basketball, he was strong, a regular guy. He was trying to stay away from girls, he told her. He already had two kids, and he was only nineteen. He'd grown up in a way she couldn't understand. He knew that.

People with some money can bury their dead or cremate them. The Lopezes were poor in grief. When Frankie's mother, Emilia, died, the funeral parlor wouldn't bury her until all the money came from social services. You can expire waiting for social services. Gay Men's Health crisis gave the family some of the money, Emilia had died of AIDS, but her embalmed body was kept over the weekend in a dismal funeral parlor on Second Avenue. The Lopezes had come to the parlor on a Friday, to take the body away, to bury Emilia, but the parlor wouldn't let them remove the body. The entire family was there, and they couldn't bury her. People with money can bury their dead. The funeral parlor charged them over four thousand dollars for a bare room and some miserly solicitousness.

Roy and Elizabeth paid their respects. The children wanted her to touch their mother's stiff body. She tried to slip a rose under the swollen hand, but she couldn't. The children, some grown, smiled at Elizabeth. Then they smiled at their young, dead mother. Emilia. She was a tenderhearted woman. Often she lived in the building, when Roy and Elizabeth had just moved in, Emilia restrained her kids from stealing their mail. They did it once or twice, but Emilia made them return it to Elizabeth. The kids liked to bust open mailboxes.

Emilia stopped them. Elizabeth rented a post office box anyway.

Elizabeth stared at Emilia's body. She didn't want to go up to the coffin. She didn't want to see vivid makeup on a dead face. She was afraid of the hand of death, its long reach. She went forward with Roy. Frankie and two of his sisters—Carmen and Susanna—wanted her there, closer to the coffin.

Frankie took Elizabeth by the hand and escorted her to it.

—Don't worry. She looks nice. Doesn't she look good?

Elizabeth thought, Death's ugly.

Frankie surveyed the mess on the sidewalk. He shook his head. He didn't become insane about the garbage and the damage. Frankie was cool. He didn't approach the morons on the church steps, he checked them out, registered who they were, for the future. He stood there, his arms folded over his chest. Then he went back inside. Frankie kept an eye on the street. He was vigilant.

Elizabeth had been inside the Lopez apartment. It was clean, it was poor, it was livable. Nothing was like Hector's apartment. Except for the apartment that was covered in talcum powder. It was in another building. Elizabeth saw it one night when the man who lived in it, a stingy man with a trust fund who drove a cab at night, wasn't in. The people who rented him the room showed it to Elizabeth. The apartment was covered in talcum powder. The floors, the bed, the dresser, the bathroom—sink, bathtub, not the toilet—were under a thick layer of white powder, piled under a carpet of talcum powder. It was hard to breathe. That apartment was worse than Hector's.

Sometimes she knocked on Hector's door. Mrs. Hector opened it a crack . Elizabeth had to pick up a package that UPS left with them. Or sometimes Elizabeth brought Mrs. Hector a blouse, if it was in good enough shape, if it was something she didn't wear anymore or never had. She'd do that rather than see it land as a reject on Hector's table.

The old dog with a human name behind Mrs. Hector growled. Mrs. Hector positioned her body to block the dog from barging out. Elizabeth could see a sliver of the apartment.

—It makes me sick.

—He's a collector, Roy said.

—Collectors are sick.

Hector collected everything, because he had nothing. People never really had what they wanted, because they wanted everything. People who could afford to buy everything were miserable about something. There's always something missing.

Things were missing in Elizabeth's life. They weren't misplaced. In any time or under any regime, it would be the same. Elizabeth couldn't replace what was lost, and what wasn't lost may never have existed to begin with. Everyone was dissatisfied, even if they didn't have much to complain about. Once deprived, always deprived.

Three men are in a nursing home. One of the men says, How old do you think I am? The two men say, Eighty-five. Everyone thinks I look eighty-five, he says proudly. But actually I'm ninety-five. He walks over to an old woman. How old do you think I am? he asks. Drop your pants, she says. and I'll tell you. He drops his pants and she grasps his penis. She fondles his penis for a while. Well, how old do you think I am? he asks. Ninety-five, she says, her hand still on his penis. How'd you know? he asks. I heard you tell the two men, she says.

When Elizabeth complained to the Big G about the state of the building, she was mindful of Hector. She didn't criticize him directly or use his name unless compelled. She tempered any criticism of Hector. She didn't want him fired, she wanted him helped or assisted. The building could be turned around. By any means possible, Roy said.

For Elizabeth's pains, the landlord and Gloria hated her. They had valid, landlord reasons. Elizabeth was white, mostly employed, though underemployed, and educated. She'd had opportunities. She was the worst kind of tenant. She wasn't as easy to push around and intimidate as people on welfare, or disadvantaged and handicapped people, or people depressed and frightened by a system that employs people to treat them with disdain while assisting them inadequately.

When a 1930s vintage stove stops working, though its oven wasn't ever regulated—if it was on, it was always 500 degrees—Elizabeth's type of tenant doesn't buy a reconditioned one on time through the landlord. With some money in the bank, her kind of tenant buys a stove for four hundred dollars rather than pay four or five dollars extra each month for the remainder of the lease, and all other leases. You pay forever for one stove. The extra money raises the base rent and increases the amount on which the next rent hike will be figured. If you have four hundred dollars, which Elizabeth and Roy did, you didn't do this. As Elizabeth explained to Gloria, It doesn't make sense to increase our rent base. Gloria's mouth fell open.

The Big G hoped to obstruct them. She'd catch Elizabeth on the street. She'd sidle over and say with a sympathetic smile, But you know you can't put that stove on the street, or she'd ask, Who's going to remove that old stove, or she'd insist, more aggressively, You'll have to

36

move it out of your apartment yourself, you know, we can't help you.

They bought a new stove anyway. They had never wanted a stove. They owned one now. This made them different from the Lopez family downstairs. The Lopezes had to pay on time.

What do you get when you cross a Mafioso with a deconstructionist?
What?
An offer you can't understand.

What do you get when you cross a Puerto Rican with a Jew?
What?
A super who thinks he owns the building.

Most of the time Elizabeth couldn't look Hector in the eye. She couldn't talk to the Big G. And nothing was accomplished. Nothing was done. Fuzzballs grew fat and fluffy in ancient grease-encrusted corners. Cigarettes and paper bags collected on the floors. It was like living in the Port Authority and paying rent.

On occasion Elizabeth phoned the housing department. Hardly anyone else did. You're not supposed to expect clean halls in the poor part of the city, or if you don't own your apartment.

—I'd like to report a violation by my landlord.
—What is your name, address, the name of the landlord? What is the complaint?
—Dirty halls.
—Where?
—The halls.

—All the halls?

—Yes. Six floors of halls and a vestibule. Sort of a vestibule. It's not really a vestibule. It's an entrance. You have to enter the building. Six halls and stairways, let's say.

—For how long has it been like this?

—Weeks and weeks. More.

—What kind of dirt? Caked-in, grease, litter?

—Yes. All kinds of dirt.

—How would you describe the dirt?

—Cigarettes, dust, blood, dope bags, loose dirt, garbage, gum, crack vials, needles, matches, paper bags, condoms, gum wrappers, hair, straws, just plain filth from weeks and weeks of people using the halls, city air is very dirty, and dust accumulates fast, you know.

Describe the dirt.

The conversation magnified the futility of having a conversation with the City. Every time she had one, which wasn't often, because she didn't want the City to think she was a lunatic, Elizabeth changed her attitude about civil servants. They were not just incompetent, unhappy, petty bureaucrats, or idiots, they were administrative sadists, sit-down comedians, they were functioning fools.

Invariably, two months later, Elizabeth would receive written notification from the City. An "Acknowledgment of Complaint" was printed on a sheet of hot pink paper.

"This acknowledges receipt of your complaint. The owner has been notified to correct this conition: Unsanitary conition in building, No lock on frnt door bldg."

The complaint had been made to the landlord. The landlord's name on the notice was not the one she'd given the Department of Housing Preservation and Development. This meant either that no complaint could've been served, because no landlord was found by that name, or that legally the landlord had a scam going and had many different names for the many buildings it owned. So who was responsible.

The other tenants were amused, bored, or surprised by her efforts. She wasn't tough or cynical enough, she wasn't hip to the way things were, the way it all worked. She'd grown up in a house in the suburbs. She'd never accept the fact that sometimes landlords don't fix buildings with tenants living in them. Some of the tenants were too numb to notice or respond, though. Some of the tenants had different expectations or no expectations. Some of the tenants thought she was an asshole. One tenant smiled at her and secretly hated the dirty floor she walked on.

Three men—a black, a WASP, and a Jew—were walking along the street. One kicked a can, and a genie appeared. The genie said, I can take all of you back to where you and your people came from. The black man said, You can take me and all my people to Africa? The genie said yes. Do it, the black man said, and he disappeared. The Jewish man asked, You can take me and all the Jews in the world to Israel? Yes, the genie said. Do it, the Jew said, and he disappeared. Then the genie turned to the WASP. The WASP said, I'll have a Diet Coke.

The street was devastated, a war zone, neutralized for the moment, like Elizabeth when she'd had too much to drink at a party and was lying on a couch, her clothes messed up, her lipstick smeared, her mouth parted, her eyes closed. The street looked like a woman who'd seen enough of life and wanted to sleep it off, push the guy away from her, go home, except she couldn't. She was home.

A few people, one at a time, were walking down the street. They dragged themselves along. A lanky guy with a jacket over his shoulder, a lounge lizard, appeared to have just come from a club or a party, maybe the one where the woman was lying on the couch. His tie was loose. Elizabeth waited to see if he scratched his arm. He didn't. Sometimes two or three drugsters walked fast down the street, stopped abruptly, huddled together, doing a deal, and one of them shouted, one of them was pissed, and one of them quieted him or her, then they moved on.

Roy woke and grunted.

—Get in bed.

—I can't.

—Get away from the window.

—No.

—Have you called the police?

—No.

—Come to sleep.

—I can't.

—What's the matter with you?

—Nothing.

Sleep was for untroubled people, the guiltless. Elizabeth didn't remember all her crimes. They went somewhere, an orphanage for abandoned crimes. Sleep was for the blameless. The shameless knew shame late at night and didn't sleep soundly. People reassured themselves with their own lies. Lies were inescapable, they were their own awful truth, necessary illusions.

Dreams tell lies that are true. The day's nightly news. Heavy sleepers escape every night. Roy did. He said dreams were the mind shining. Elizabeth couldn't escape, and she couldn't remember what she was escaping. She sat near the fire escape. She watched the amorphous street. It absorbed everything, her attention, her tension. She could run away. She didn't want to go anywhere. Everywhere was wrong. She was a native, she was restless and reckless. She was also fickle and impulsive. And sometimes she was very bad.

Elizabeth yawned. She wasn't sure if she was hungry.

Outside, a bad drug deal was accompanied by outrage and howls of anger.

—You get what? You shittin' me, you better not fuck me, man, this is bad shit, man. Don't take me for no fool. You dissin' me, man, don't dis me, man, I'll kill you.

She expected one of them to pull a gun any second, except another dealer ran all the way down the block from the corner. He grabbed the arm of the screaming one and pulled him away, pulled him down the block, still screaming.

—You dissin' me, I'm gonna cap you.

Junkies and junkie dealers were active, busy. They had something to do, somewhere to go, someone to meet, they were always meeting someone, somewhere, and they had something to take care of every minute of the day. It wasn't the best life, a life stripped of everything but the substance they craved and would become sick without, it was life though. All their needs were contained in one little plastic bag, and they could buy different-colored bags. They didn't have to consider what they'd like to do each day. They knew what they liked and what they had to do. Even rich junkies had to score. It wasn't like buying a pack of cigarettes or a bottle of alcohol. It occupied them, totally, she saw it on their faces.

Some middle-class junkies sold her a rug, and when she handed the guy a twenty, any pretense at civility slid off his expectant, sweaty face, and he grabbed the bill, jacked up the price by five dollars— it was still a deal because they'd probably stolen the carpet from their parents. They said they were poor. They couldn't wait another minute, they'd take any amount of money for something that was worth more. Elizabeth handed him the twenty too easily. He could get another five. The way he grabbed the twenty out of her hand, the way he didn't say thanks, the way he and his friend—a woman as ragged and dragged—looked at each other, they had enough to score, get straight, get well, whatever, it was a dramatic, insular moment, all to itself, extreme.

Money had a single purpose. Junkies were relentlessly goal-oriented. Misguided achievers were joined by their need, and that need united rich and poor the way nothing else did. One night she walked behind a rich and a poor junkie. The rich one was in a wrinkled Armani suit, the poor one wore greasy black jeans. Their heads were close, they were perspiring and bonded, brothers in addiction.

The street addict stage-whispered to the rich addict:

—Man, he took a look at your threads, and he raised the price a hundred.

They slouched along and consoled each other, the rich guy apologizing, but it didn't matter, because they'd scored, they were just talking until they could shoot up.

Elizabeth didn't want to care about everything.

A Jewish grandmother is walking along Jones Beach with her grandson. A big wave comes along and sweeps her grandson out to sea. The old woman gets down on her knees and prays to God. please, God, give me back my grandson. I'll do anything. Please give my boy back to me. She wails and moans and suddenly a big wave crests and at the top of it is her grandson. He lands at her feet. The grandmother looks up at the sky and says, He had a hat.

She suffered fools, landlords, enemies, and junkies. She had to wait around for similar and dissimilar male and female junkies to get up from the vestibule floor, after they'd slumped there, after they'd shot up, she had to wait for them to get off the floor of the dark vestibule almost every night. They left blood on the floor, bright red dots of blood. caught in the act, they lied to her. They weren't shooting up. They were waiting for someone to come home.

—We're waiting for Cathy.

—There's no Cathy. You're going to shoot up.

They'd struggle to stuff their paraphernalia back in a bag and pull themselves up from the floor. They'd agree to leave. They'd walk past Elizabeth.

—We're just being nice, because there is a Cathy.

Some cleaned up after themselves, not because they were neat. If they left no trace of their works and bloody business, they could return. Some attempted permanent invisibility. They were spectral characters. They were young and drained of life, they were alone, desperate, and hollow. Elizabeth didn't want them there, she didn't want to walk over them, and she hated seeing the blood on the floor and on their legs as they furtively rushed to cover the place where they'd just shot up.

One of them was asleep. She was about sixteen, blond, cute. Elizabeth woke her. She was sprawled on the floor. Elizabeth couldn't open the door and get inside her own building. The girl roused herself finally.

—Don't you have a home? Elizabeth asked.

Elizabeth delivered the question like a guidance counselor or social worker. The girl was stunned. Someone didn't think she had a home. The girl didn't know how low she'd sunk in someone else's eyes, how she looked to someone else. You need other people to feel humiliated. I have a home, she said truculently. She slunk away and moved dejectedly down the street like a wounded baby animal.

A friend of Roy's told him a story. The friend was a reformed or recovering addict. One night when he was still getting high, he was waiting on line in a drug store, a hole in the wall farther east. A woman behind him said, Isn't it funny? The more I do, the more I want. Roy's friend repeated the story to Roy. His friend said, she didn't know she was a junkie. Roy wasn't surprised by that. He thought people were stupid.

Junkies in the vestibule every night or every other night and puddles of blood and tiny scraps of tissue with blood on them and round little bright red drops of blood on the stairs were part of her environment. Junkies liked the vestibule. It was cool. The door and vestibule situation was another fight Elizabeth had with the Big G.

Elizabeth phoned at least five times, over any year, suggesting in a pleasant voice into the landlord's answering machine—they never picked up—various ways to keep junkies out.

—Hello, this is Elizabeth Hall. I'd like to discuss the junkies in the vestibule. If you would just give us a lock on the outer door, and place the intercom on the outside, or, and this would be less expensive, a glass door or a heavy plastic door, or even cheaper, as an alternative, cut out panels from the bottom of the existing door. . .

No one phoned her back.

Elizabeth noticed other front doors along her block. All of them were made of thick glass. That way junkies couldn't hide and stick needles into old collapsed veins or new bouncy ones. They couldn't slump on the floor and disappear. They weren't the disappeared. They were visible behind glass. They were as visible as on the street. But sometimes, even on the street, they huddled close together like Russians on the steppes and stuck needles into their arms, sheltering each other under blankets or stained coats.

The crackheads didn't leave blood in the vestibule. They left plastic vials and sometimes plastic cups of water. They were bloody, though, erratic and hostile. One of them said, when Elizabeth insisted they get off the floor and leave the vestibule, so she could open the door and get inside, one of them said, with deep sarcasm:

—You're some human being.

Elizabeth wanted to strangle the peroxided, stringy-haired creature, with her disastrously thin legs and arms, and a face that betrayed every bad night she'd ever had. Elizabeth wanted to knock her senseless, not that she had any. The peroxided creature might one night come to her senses, she might look in a car's mirror, twist it to see her ravaged face. Elizabeth couldn't see what she'd see. People make the best of a bad situation.

Elizabeth preferred heroin users to crackheads. Everyone did. Crackheads were erratic. Her preference was irrelevant. She would've preferred never to work.

The poor scrambled, adapted, and metamorphosed into their poverty. They grew ugly. The rich grew ugly too. Repellent. They were complacent. Elizabeth hated that complacent, unearned well-being. Complacency was the rich glow on their faces. They believed in their right to their wealth. The glow made them ugly. Poor people never glowed. Ugliness is more than skin deep. They ate up their poverty, the way the rich ate up their plenty. The poor digested meagerness and cramped quarters, and even if some of them were Catholic and preached to about God's loving the poor more than the rich, they were living in the U.S.A. People lived the lives they deserved.

Now one of the morons stood up and vomited. He vomited all over the sidewalk. He made gut-wrenching noises to roars of moronic approval. Elizabeth lost her appetite. One of the other morons threw some food at a store window. The drug store windows all displayed Tide and Ajax, which signaled they didn't sell anything but drugs. Idiots or gringos went in and asked for milk.

The morons bellowed again and held some kind of vomit-and-garbage-throwing ceremony. Glass broke. Stones and bottles were tossed. They screamed happily, unimportantly. Her mother would say like banshees. Elizabeth wondered what a banshee sounded like.

The taste of vomit was in her mouth. Vomit was putrid longing backing up.

She wanted to be able to stop the morons. She couldn't do everything she wanted.

He vomited again. He probably liked to vomit.

She'd been able to stop some girls. She persuaded them to stop blasting music from their car. It was parked under her window. They were doing their laundry across the street. It was a dope Jeep. Elizabeth dressed and walked downstairs. Roy told her not to. She knocked on the Jeep's half-open window. The driver didn't hear anything. Elizabeth had to touch her on the shoulder. The driver turned to her.

—Could you please turn down? My baby can't sleep, Elizabeth said.

The girl did instantly, out of a traditional respect for babies and motherhood. Elizabeth walked away, aware of the girls in the Jeep studying her and doubting that she was a mother. They didn't turn up again.

How many New Yorkers does it take to screw in a lightbulb?
None of your fucking business.

How many performance artists does it take to screw in a lightbulb?
I don't know. I left early.

She could easily pretend to be a mother. She couldn't see herself going into Paragon Sporting Goods, asking to look at crossbows and arrows. Before she did anything, Elizabeth saw herself doing it. If she was going to walk down the stairs, she saw herself walking down the stairs. She saw herself taking the first step. She prepared herself. Her heel might catch in the hem of her pants, and she'd hurtle forward and crash, land on her head. She could decide to jump, lunge, leap, or fly over the stairs. She thought she could fly over a flight of stairs. It looked easy. She didn't want to train for years to be able to do it. That was crazy.

She wouldn't murder the morons in cold blood or in a moment of passion. When she murdered, it would be in self-defense. She'd be attacked. A large man or a small man would come at her. From behind. She'd move quickly, swing around. She'd gouge out his eyes or jab her fingers into his gut. She wanted to be able to sever someone's jugular vein or hit someone over the head with the baseball bat Roy kept near the door. She'd bash the aggressor to death without blinking an eye. Then she'd toss the bloody bat onto the floor and phone the precinct.

I just murdered a man with a bat. Right, a bat. He's bleeding, but he's dead. Don't send an ambulance. Dead. A bat. A baseball bat.

Even her revenge fantasies were silly. They ended without conviction. She clenched her hands into fists. She watched Roy sleeping. He was sleeping the sleep of the just and unjust and the innocent and the guilty.

She followed the band of morons with tired eyes. They sauntered toward the park. They turned over another garbage can in a blasé way. Threw one at a car. They'd had a lot of experience throwing and overturning garbage cans. They turned over the last one casually, even gracefully, with a little wrist action. They could be tennis players or garbage collectors. There was garbage everywhere. It wouldn't be picked up.

On her block, the garbage collectors left as much garbage on the streets as they picked up. They threw the garbage cans all over the sidewalks. It was a display of real disgust, gutter hatred of the poor. Elizabeth caught them doing it.

On another night she couldn't sleep, she went downstairs at six A.M., carrying newspapers to be recycled. The garbagemen were throwing garbage and garbage cans. The street was an ordinary disaster, strewn with evidence of rampaging dogs or mad people. She wished she had her camera. But the garbagemen could argue about the photographs. They'd get lawyers, they'd interpret it their way. Her block wasn't covered in garbage, it was her point of view, how she saw things, she had a distorted view of the world, of the block, they'd say. She did.

They'd say the garbage collectors couldn't have done it, because they were on their coffee break. Some hooligans must've done it, they fled before anyone saw them. Elizabeth could spend her life in court defending herself, her story. She'd present her story, and one of the garbagemen would say, That's not the way it was. He'd shake his head adamantly or sadly, as if the thought of his doing something like that was beyond him. I would never do something like that, he'd insist dramatically. Maybe he'd cry. The jury would side with the men in uniform. Elizabeth would be branded a fanatic, an urban malcontent. She remembered the garbagemen down the street in their uniforms. She remembered their faces. She remembered thinking, I pay taxes to the City for them to take away garbage.

It was pathetic. she watched as they flung the last cans onto the sidewalk. She surveyed the devastation and then glared at the men. She memorized their truck's number. She was overwhelmed by despair. she noticed the acerbic super down the other end of the block. His face was inflamed, scarlet. Sometimes his face looked tanned and healthy, sometimes like an old shoe. She walked over to him, he always knew everything, who was in jail, who was about to go to jail and why, when there was going to be a bust. Elizabeth announced that she was going to report the garbage collectors.

—What'd they look like? A tall black guy and a short Italian guy? The regular guys are OK. These aren't the regular guys. The regular guys are good guys. They wouldn't do this.

He gestured to the street. They both looked at it.

—Are they rogue garbage collectors? Elizabeth asked.

The acerbic super and Elizabeth laughed in the morbid morning air. Morning is for mourning, Elizabeth thought. Another garbage truck rolled along and disgorged the regular guys. They were doing the other side of the street. Elizabeth walked over to the short Italian one.

—Take a look at our block. It looks worse than it did last night. Look at the garbage everywhere, look at the cans all over the sidewalk. How can they do this and call themselves garbage collectors?

The regular garbage collector surveyed the sidewalk. He saw the randomness, the mayhem, the sidewalk littered haphazardly with black plastic and aluminum cans. He saw the Chinese food, milk cartons, dog shit, cat food cans, and diapers scattered contemptuously on the ground. The regular guy hurried. He raced to make things right, to turn the cans right side up. He shouted, as he ran, that he'd take care of it. He didn't want her to report them. He didn't want trouble. She didn't report all the wrong things she saw. It was depressing and time-consuming.

Elizabeth opened the window wide. She didn't care who saw. The morons were crossing Avenue A. They were dancing. A speeding cop car or an ambulance racing to save someone could hit them. They might be killed or they could all be murdered in the park by a crackhead. Her mother said, Where there's life, there's hope. She didn't want to die, she told Elizabeth, because there's no future in death.

The third-floor man was still in his window across the street. Even with his lights off, his dark shape filled the window. Elizabeth saw something. It could've been his dog. Roy was still sleeping peacefully, and she hated and loved him for it. He was missing the night's frantic errors. Strident, bizarre noises didn't wake him.

The third-floor man's lack of acknowledgment creeped her out. But she didn't want to wave to him. That demanded a leap across a great chasm, her acknowledging his looking at her. She felt little, belittled. She shrank back.

A series of high-pitched yelps or squeals started. They seemed to come from someplace close. It sounded like someone was being tortured. Roy didn't move. He was a smooth stone on the bed. He didn't look alive. Elizabeth couldn't figure out if the torture noises came from human beings, dogs, or cats. People tortured their animals. They tortured their children. children tortured animals. Everyone's a monster, given the opportunity.

She was sure the man was watching her from his window. It was obvious. He was pretending he wasn't. She didn't want to hide.

She was covered, decent, whatever. He wasn't hiding. But she wasn't watching him. He could think she was. It was a dilemma. She wanted to watch the street, not him, but she couldn't watch the street without the possibility that he would think she was watching him. Even her freedom or opportunity—her liberty to look out a window—was controlled by others. She didn't want to give in and leave the window.

Acknowledgment could disarm the situation, him, but it could also trigger harm, attack.

He was probably the kind of man who made sucking noises when he ate and slept, when he fucked. He smacked his lips when he chewed and food drool poured from the corners of his thin lips. He opened his mouth wide, and you could see the food inside and the spittle dribbling out of his mouth, and he had a grin on his face like an idiot, but jesus he loved to eat.

She wouldn't acknowledge him.

Maybe he knew he was a creep. Maybe creeps know they're condemned for life. Maybe he was the kind of man who shaves close, nicks his skin and wears cheap, cloying aftershave lotion, who slaps it on and thinks it covers his sins. Maybe he hated himself.

Some people who hate themselves wear perfume. Elizabeth liked certain perfumes and others made her sick. She didn't hate herself all the time. She hated herself less when she liked her own smell. But she didn't want it to be overpowering. It was hard enough to visit people in their apartments or ride in a taxi driven by a maniac who didn't know his way around. Some people burned incense day and night or wore sickeningly sweet perfume. Some taxi drivers hung furry green-and-white odor-eaters from rearview mirrors. Elizabeth often became nauseated.

—You smell good, she told Roy yesterday.

—That'll change, he said.

The morons were gone. The block was a moron-free zone. She was free. Elizabeth liked her block. She felt possessive about it. She liked her apartment.

A horse goes into a bar and sits down.
The bartender asks, Why the long face?

When the landlord was about to raise the rent, Elizabeth received a letter. All the tenants did. The landlord stated that because they'd given the tenants new windows, which weren't put in right, they'd measured wrong, because they'd replaced the old mailbox, which had been broken since she'd moved in, and because they'd put in a light in the front hallway, which was required by law, the landlord regretfully was raising the rent a certain amount per room for every tenant. The landlord assessed the number of rooms at two more than Elizabeth thought she had.

Elizabeth shoved the letter under a stack of junk mail. She ignored it for a day. Then she took it out. She did the figuring. She added up her rooms and multiplied to find what it would cost monthly. It wasn't astronomical. She could live with it or die with it. She might do both. She wasn't going to fight it. Fight the increase. The phrase appealed to her—fight the increase. It was what she should do. But she wasn't going to, not after Gloria had insulted her. Six dollars more per room for the rest of her life, even for rooms she didn't have, was better than standing in a poorly ventilated room next to Gloria.

Being reasonable with the Big G was murder.

Roy read the letter. He thought they should do something. He glanced at Elizabeth and shoved the paper over to her side of the table.

—I can't rouse myself to action, she said.

—Rouse yourself to inaction, he said.

—No.

—Answer the letter. Do something.

—I can't. You do it. Do something yourself.

—I don't do that kind of thing.

—Why not?

—It's beneath me.

—I don't do floors, either.

Their upstairs neighbor was aroused. Ernest was an actor. He worked in a bookstore. Ernest shoved a letter under their door one night. It was addressed to her. He wanted to discuss the tenant situation, their position. Long sentences covered the unlined paper. He said he wanted Elizabeth's help in fighting the rent increase. He used the compelling phrase. He followed his letter with a telephone message that took up five minutes on her answering machine. They'd never even talked or seen each other in the hallway. She hadn't seen him. She'd heard him above her, she'd heard what she thought were his footsteps. He exercised.

Then Ernest showed up, after the note and call. He was likable. He told her that when he read the landlord's letter, he went berserk. He couldn't sleep, he was infuriated by the injustice, the lies. He wanted to take the landlord on, with her assistance. He'd do the hard work, the field work, go to City Hall, search for the building plans, for the architectural drawings. He just wanted her assistance.

The same letter that swamped her in lethargy was the key to an ignition switch in Ernest. Indignant, he enlisted Elizabeth. She was inert and apathetic. But he knew, somehow, that she of all the tenants would be open to his plea. He may have heard her walking late at night, heard in her gait some telltale sign of anxiety. Maybe he even discerned in it a desire for a better world, for justice. That was impossible, she supposed. It was probably because she was friendlier than most of the other tenants. Maybe he had seen her in the hallway and she'd smiled, unaware of who he was. Yes, OK, I will, she said finally. He was asking next to nothing of her.

She would make a few phone calls, knock on tenant doors, get some names on their petition. She'd help write letters, do some minor evidence gathering, contact various City agencies only by phone if he asked her to. She'd use her proofreader's expertise on the letters. The letters would spell doom, defeat, for the landlord's illegal hopes. Elizabeth told Ernest that she'd make sure there weren't any errors of fact or grammar in the letters, no typos. Elizabeth would see to their correctness. The landlord had applied for MCIs, Major Capital Improvements, Ernest explained. They were requesting more than they deserved. They wouldn't get it, he said.

They spent time together, side by side, strategizing. They had to determine how the landlord should be rebutted and combated and what information they needed. The landlord stated that their building and the one next door were one building. That way any repairs on the one next door counted as money spent on their building. Their building could be charged higher rents for work done on the other building. An evil-twin situation, Elizabeth thought. She'd once wanted to be a twin, but now it repulsed her. The two buildings' separate registrations had to be found. The other building had double the number of tenants too, double the trouble.

Ernest was relentless. He was on fire. He went downtown to a vast City building. He walked through room after room and floor after floor, through hundreds of rooms of file cabinets and computers and documents. He dealt with clerical people who ignored him. He waited on long lines and wasted his life. Elizabeth read that people waited on line at the post office five years of their lives. Waiting added up. Then Ernest would get to the head of the line and as part of a tradition or ritual he would be told he was on the wrong line and he should see another clerical person, somewhere else, on another floor or building, and that person would keep him waiting too, be rude, or tell him to see someone else and finally someone else would tell him he or she couldn't help him, and he had to start all over, in another location, on another line. He did that. Elizabeth was impressed. He took action. He was a hero in a local way.

Ernest even found a free tenant lawyer. He came back from the first meeting with pages of yellow paper; he'd taken detailed notes. He absorbed and learned acronyms for all the City agencies and departments, and he learned legal terms too. Elizabeth didn't know exactly what the acronyms stood for. Since Ernest did, she didn't need to. A PAR, he repeated patiently, was a Petition for Administrative Review.

A man was going away and he asked his brother to look after his cat. Then he phoned home to ask how the cat was. The brother answered, Your cat is dead. The first brother asked, How can you tell me like that? Why didn't you prepare me? You could've said,

Your cat ran away. I'll look for it. Call back in a day. Then when I called back, you could've said, The cat's on the roof. And the next time I called, then you could've told me the cat was dead. You should've prepared me. His brother said he was sorry. Some years later, the man went away again. He called his brother. He asked, How's Mom? His brother said, She's on the roof.

Ernest asked Elizabeth to attend one of the legal sessions with him. The office wasn't far, and the meeting wouldn't take much of her time, he said. Elizabeth agreed, shamed by his commitment. The meeting was in a shabby brown room, with fake wood furniture. The lawyer wasn't a lawyer but a paralegal she used the acronyms Ernest used and knew. MCI. PAR. Elizabeth tried to appear involved. She knew if this was a documentary she'd be caught looking uninterested. There were stacks of paper on the harassed woman's desk, thousands of claims against landlords, standing for thousands of tenants in trouble. It was a sorry place for sorry situations. Elizabeth was desperate in desperate places. Hector the super's daughter-in-law walked in to the squalid office. Elizabeth said hello, and everyone nodded. Hector's daughter-in-law was having trouble with her landlord and her husband. Elizabeth knew that. She'd already had two kids and the two kids were miserable. Even before their parents separated, the kids were falling on their faces, having too many awful accidents, and were being rushed, bloody, to too many emergency rooms. The daughter-in-law was tragic at eighteen.

Elizabeth worried that the girl would mention seeing them to Hector the super, seeing them in the free tenant lawyer's office. Hector would tell the Big G. Ernest told Elizabeth they were within their rights, doing what they were doing, they were absolutely within their rights. Nothing would happen to them. He smiled benignly at her.

Elizabeth wasn't sure if being within her rights covered being seen as a conspirator, an agitator, and whether her rights would keep her from being tormented before being thrown out of the building illegally in the middle of the night. It wouldn't happen, Ernest went on reassuringly. They were sitting tenants with leases. She was, she repeated to herself, a sitting tenant with a lease.

One night, when no one was around, except the morons on the street, Ernest and Elizabeth collected evidence for their dossier against the landlord. Pictures had to be included with the letter to the city. They needed photographs of the filthy halls, walls, and broken stairs. It was so late, the building was quiet, like the Tombs, Ernest said grimly. They arranged to meet in front of her door. They moved stealthily through the halls. They skulked. The naked lightbulbs were stark illumination. The light accented the streaks on the walls. Shadows made it harder to know where the dirt was and also made the dark spots darker. It was just the way shadows in gangster and romantic movies obscure and enhance the seamy sides of life.

The joke was that they needed photographs of holes in the floor. Any one of the tenants could have tripped or caught their heel in the ugly recesses, they could have fallen down and broken their nose. They could have fallen down and in a freak accident died because of the way their head hit the floor. If they were drunk, they could have tripped, hit their head, and bled to death on the floor. The tenants could've sued the landlord. Elizabeth thought the landlord would've wanted to repair things, to avoid being sued. But if everyone's too

58

poor to get lawyers, or too intimidated, why should the landlord repair anything, or if people like her—whatever that meant—couldn't even respond when their rent was being raised unfairly, then landlords didn't have to fix anything. She'd heard about someone who broke his arm falling out of bed to answer the phone, though his bed was on the floor. Accidents happen all the time.

The ugliest hole was in the deepest shadow. It was too dark in the vestibule to take pictures. The light overhead was the dangling naked bulb that the landlord had recently put in, the one they wanted the tenants to pay extra rent for every month. It was weak. If anyone wanted to mug you in the small vestibule, you'd never see him well enough to identify him. The weak light wasn't a deterrent in any way. Just the opposite. Ernest and Elizabeth were standing very close to each other in the small entryway. She could feel his anxiety. She liked it and hated it.

—I need more light, Elizabeth said.

—You don't have a good enough view? Ernest asked.

—I can see the hole with my eyes, but it won't come out on the photograph.

—Let me open the door, he said.

He opened the front door as wide as it would go. Then he studied her with a worried expression.

—Is that better?

Is that better? she thought. The way he said, Let me open the door, his perplexity about photographing the hole, the way he said, Is that better? was priceless and ridiculous at the same time. She fell in love with him. For a minute. He changed in her eyes in the dark, ugly vestibule.

She could fall in love with anyone.

He was still holding the front door open so she could get a better shot of the hole. She knew the picture wouldn't come out. It was close to hopeless, futile. The City might still be impressed by the documentation. They also had to get photographs of loose tiles and grease in the corners. There was a stair that slid out by itself, and anyone could slip off and kill themselves, it just came out, but it was hard to take a picture of that. They moved the stair to show that it was loose, to show it in its improper, dangerous position. Photographing dust on the walls was implausible. She did it anyway and looked at Ernest. He was smiling, reassuringly. He knew it was absurd. He wasn't deluded, he was optimistic. Ernest was a mystery.

She looked at his mouth. She had never noticed the thin scar on his chin. Maybe he'd been in a duel. He was a swashbuckler for tenants' rights. She could fall in love with anyone if the timing was right and the place was right, or wrong. If she was in a room long enough with someone, with no other people around, or if she was trapped in a place, she could fall in love with anyone. Like an animal. She liked animals. They were adaptable.

Anyone could fall in love with anyone, under the right circumstances. Maybe it was the survival instinct. Elizabeth wasn't sure she had one. People wanted to continue themselves, protect themselves, get pleasure. People wanted pleasure all the time, anytime, anyplace, they'd do anything to get it. Everyone was capable of the most hideous behavior and crimes to get it. The pursuit of pleasure wasn't pretty. It made people cruel during tender moments. If they weren't really getting what they wanted, they could kill as easily as kiss.

Ernest was driven. Driven was sex to her, sexy. Someone active and alive with desire for anything was sexy. Maybe not driven for a car, or ice cream, or heroin, because it excluded you, the possibility of you. she could kind of tell what somebody was like sexually, what their body might act like if stimulated, from the way they wanted supposedly nonsexual things. Nothing wasn't sexual.

Ernest and Elizabeth finished for the night. They had done the job. The Polaroids were flat and weird, but they were evidence. They showed something. Maybe the City would appreciate that.

Hillary and Bill Clinton are driving around. They stop at a gas station. Hillary gets out and talks a long time to the gas station attendant. Finally she gets back into the car. Bill says, Who was that? Hillary says, He's an old boyfriend of mine. Bill says, A gas station attendant? Hillary says, If I'd married him, he would've been president.

Now Elizabeth wasn't exactly seeing as she stared out the window. Things were moving, even imperceptibly. She couldn't live without windows. She got bored easily. She needed outside stimulation. She even wanted the outside inside her.

The street looked like desolation alley.

A man walks into a bar. He sits down and places a gunnysack on the barstool next to him. It starts to move. The bartender says, What's that? What's in there? I don't want any animals in here. Get it out of here. The guy says, It's not an animal. Listen, I'll show it to you if you give me a drink. It's really amazing. OK, says the bartender, but it better not be an animal. The guy opens the gunnysack and a little man about twelve inches high jumps out. He looks around and sees the piano. He runs to it and begins to play. He plays beautifully. The bartender is astounded. He's great, says the bartender, I've never seen anything like that. The guy says, Well, one day I met a gypsy woman, and she gave me a ring. She said, Rub the ring and make a wish, and I'll give you whatever you ask for. But you have to be very careful about your pronunciation, because I didn't ask for a twelve-inch pianist.

The moon was fading. The sun was starting to rise. It showed the top of its fierce face. It rose resolutely. Daily Elizabeth negotiated with nature. Anything natural was a problem.

Elizabeth did contact other tenants, she did what Ernest asked her to do. One of the tenants was hard of hearing. Before she knew he was deaf, she tried phoning him. She raised her voice higher and higher and then she shouted into the phone and then hung up. She met him briefly on the street. She realized he couldn't hear a word she was saying unless she stood in front of him so he could see her mouth move, and in addition she shouted. He was stone deaf. She didn't know why he had a phone. Then she sent him a letter.

*Dear Herbert,*

*I would like to talk to you about our protest against the rent hike the landlord is proposing.*

*We are filing our objections to the Major Capital Improvements and would like to know your objections. We know that a former tenant in your apartment did file a PAR, Petition for Administrative Review, a while ago, but we do not* know what the specific protest was—windows? a hallway problem? Do you know? Did you file anything? Do you have any evidence or documents about the building's condition?

Others in your building have also filed. If you could be of any help contacting them and finding out their objections, please let us know as soon as you can.

You and I say hello on the street. Because you are hard of hearing, the phone is not the best way to communicate. Let's meet in front of the building when it's convenient. Please contact me or Ernest—he's in in the mornings. We both have answering machines or actually you could drop a line, just send me a letter. Please contact us any way you wish. If you can't reach people in your building, Ernest and I will write letters. But are the people who filed still living there? I couldn't find any of them listed in the phone book.

Many thanks.

Sincerely, Elizabeth Hall


Elizabeth worried that mentioning his deafness would offend him. She wasn't going to pretend that screaming into the phone was easy or adequate. They had to communicate. Herbert responded. Maybe he wasn't sensitive or maybe she hadn't offended him. He was accustomed to being deaf. He was used to the stupidities of the nondeaf. He was happy to help, he said, when they met, face to face, in front of the building. She thought he said that, or that's what she heard, because he didn't pronounce words clearly. She had to interpret. She may have confused his complaints for others he didn't have. She shouted her thanks, and they shook hands. He helped Ernest and her contact some other tenants in his building.

Ernest and Elizabeth went to see one of them. He lived in the alleged same building as theirs. Architecturally it had been the same—Roy said she was going to see how the other half lived. The other half had been a mirror image, but the landlord recently halved all the apartments. Then reconditioned them. The ceilings were lower and made of a porous material. The apartments smelled bad. They lacked proportion. They were hopeless, shapeless.

His apartment had no outside or available light. It was probably illegal to have just one window looking out on a wall. Elizabeth could hardly breathe. The place was a hole, in a desperate condition. The guy was cute, even handsome. Elizabeth knew that no one would expect the condition he lived in from the way he looked. It was like the super Hector's apartment, though she'd never had the chance to enter Hector's. It was smaller than Hector's and the cute guy was the only person in it. All the shit was his.

To him, it meant nothing. She could see that. His surroundings meant nothing to him. There could have been decades of vomit caked on the walls and floors, he wouldn't have noticed. He didn't see it or smell it. He must have also been like Hector in that way, except he was a rock musician, not a super. The decals on his guitar case announced his seat in the theater of life. Lobster of Hate was the decal she liked best. She'd heard them play.

People live in very strange conditions. People live in situations no one talks about. People live in ways no one sees. People live in ways that aren't described and have to be forgotten if they are. People live in ways that no one wants to hear about or can accept, so no one hears about them, no one's told, no one listens. No one would believe the descriptions. TV sitcoms were descriptions of a very few situations. All situations might ultimately be comedies, but all comedies and situations weren't on television. So few of them surfaced, so few situations ever lit up the screen, everything was predictable.

The cute guy's place wasn't predictable, not from the way he looked. It wasn't that unusual either, except no one talked about it. People live like this voluntarily. People are free to live like this.

Ernest took notes on the yellow pad while the cute guy talked. Ernest was stable and winning. Elizabeth wandered mentally while Ernest talked to the guy. He was collecting information for their dossier to the City. That was their agenda.

She was collecting other information. She was taking her own notes. She was looking around. She was taking in the guy and his place. It was hard. But she found a way not to be there. She wasn't fucking the cute musician in her head, she couldn't bring herself to do it, with him and Ernest in the room. Instead she saw the girl he'd brought back from a club, it was very late, and they were both high, drunk, stoned, and he opens his door, and the girl gasps, she has an asthma attack because of the years of dust, so they never fuck. Or, maybe they do fuck, she's really turned on by the shit they're fucking in, she's from a strict family in the Midwest, or from an upstate New York farm, and she's never seen anything like this, and she thinks it's romantic. Elizabeth couldn't remember if she found this scene romantic when she was twenty. Fucking on dirty clothes. She was too old to be young, couldn't revive her adolescence like a comeback career. She didn't think she'd be rejuvenated by fucking him. She could imagine it. The smells would be the same, the actions would be the same, nothing would be changed. But she was older. She was going to grow even older, old, and she was going to become less flexible and drier and more indifferent and she'd eventually become decrepit no matter who or what she fucked, and then she would breathe her last breath and expire. It was inevitable.

The cute guy had filed a complaint with the City once, he told them. Ernest and Elizabeth had him sign his name to their petition. It felt like success. Then they started to leave. The cute guy said to Elizabeth, How's about getting together again and talking about the situation? Ernest shot Elizabeth a look. Elizabeth said, Whatever, I mean, whatever Ernest wants. . . . She pretended she didn't realize what kind of situation he had in mind. She wondered if Ernest was jealous. Ernest never referred to it. Ernest had deep reserves.

The other tenants never materialized, they never answered Elizabeth's carefully crafted letters. They could have been eliminated, through intimidation for one thing. It was not out of the question—Elizabeth could imagine it—that the renovations started and the tenants, the complaining ones, were not told when the walls were going to be torn down, because the Big G hated them, the way she hated Elizabeth, a little less, and some were lying in bed and the walls fell on them, so their legs were broken, or they were buried under the debris or in a wall. A cryptic end in a tenement crypt. Improbable.

They were eliminated because the noise of construction, the daily crash and boom, drove them out, drove them screaming into the night, or, when the walls came down, and the vermin came out and bit them, the tenants' legs became swollen and inflamed and covered in red itchy wounds, and, marked by disease, they fled, yelling about bugs and rats, about hardy roaches. They were driven out, and the landlord could raise the rent. Or the drilling and banging every day ended their relationships, decimated their tenuous loves, and they broke up, broke their leases, or they developed respiratory illnesses,

66

living in dust for months, and they fled their homes, and the landlord had its way, forced them out. The landlord could raise the rent the way it planned, and the landlord did raise the rent on the smaller, blighted apartments, on the newly fixed-up, reconditioned hovels.

That was a while ago.

Two women are at a hotel in the Catskills. One says, The food is terrible here. Yes, the other says, and there's so little of it.

Now a few people were leaving their floor-throughs or one-bedrooms, or studio apartments, to go to work. The blue collars. The housekeepers. The train conductors. The nurses. Some people were coming home. The prostitutes, the bartenders, the club managers, the clubgoers, the musicians, the alcoholics, the night people. There weren't as many of them as those going to day jobs. There were several taxi drivers.

One night a taxi—a checker—was parked across the street. Elizabeth noticed some movement in the front seat. She couldn't tell what it was. She watched. The driver was getting a blow job. The prostitute's head went up and down, up and down, up and down. Then it stopped, the movement stopped, and, like an animal stuck in the mud, the taxi driver, who was large, rolled over and lay on top of the poor prostitute.

The taxi driver had a huge ass. The moon was out, a full moon, and the moon lit his ass, spotlighted it. If it was done in the movies, no one would believe it.

He starts to fuck her and his big white ass, all lit up, goes up and down, up and down, up and down.

Three people come out of the front door of a building. Two men, one woman, maybe coming from a party, maybe they'd had a menage a trois. They looked preppy. Maybe they'd had coffee. one of the men immediately spots the taxi driver's big ass humping up and down, up and down, the moon shining on it, but he doesn't want the woman to see. He positions himself between her and the taxi. But finally they all see it. The three stand there, spellbound on the sidewalk, watching until the taxi driver comes. Then the driver sits up, the prostitute sits up, and he starts the car and drives away.

The hooker was probably from the next corner. It was before AIDS hit big-time. There were a lot more hookers on the next block. They all had habits and most of them were gone now, dead. The serial murderer Joel Rilkin killed at least one of them. The mother of one of the murdered hookers said in the *Times*, "Think of her as a girl, my daughter, not just as a whore." There were always ripe, new working girls. They faded fast.

It was pretty late the night Elizabeth and Ernest left the cute guy's hideous hole. But that night, and it was the only one, Ernest and Elizabeth went for a serious cup of coffee in a nearby cafe. Elizabeth's regular, the Pick Me Up.

Even though it was late and cold, the crusties—that's what Roy called them—weren't far away. They were never far away. They were lying on the street near the Pick Me up with their dogs and their dogs' puppies. Elizabeth liked the puppies. They would be raised to be vicious. The crusties were probably already training them to go for people's throats when they didn't give them money. The crusties thought of themselves as road warriors, except they never moved, they sat or lay on the sidewalk, and then in a group they'd move off,

68

they never walked alone, they were terrified kids who talked shit to everyone in the neighborhood, they looked miserable, they smelled terrible, they didn't shower even in the summer, so their piercings became infected. Except for a few of the females who retained surprisingly old-fashioned feminine wiles, all the others smelled of things no one wanted to get near.

The crusties spit at people who walked on the sidewalk near them. You went out to get a newspaper in the morning, and even if you didn't look at them, which Elizabeth didn't, she never looked at them if she could help it, they made nasty comments and spit. She was walking behind a guy in shorts. He passed the crusties, and one said to the other, Let's kill him. The guy stumbled, completely weirded out. The crusties weren't liked on the block or in the neighborhood, not even by other so-called outlaws. They spit at people in the morning before they were barely awake. They said things like, Let's kill him, for no reason. They pretended to be squatters. They were nothing, and there was nothing to them. If you open your eyes, get dressed, walk outside to get a cup of coffee, and someone spits at you for no reason, first thing, the spitter is nothing, doesn't deserve to live. Not everyone does. Elizabeth wouldn't even talk about it.

Elizabeth never gave the crusties money. She gave other people money. Tyrone who hung around the building, a nameless woman with a nameless dog, Earl who was up from the south, permanently jobless, and the Hispanic guy with a patch over his eye, those two alternated duty at the post office, manned the door with cups in hand. But she never gave the crusties money. Even though they had dogs. It was a gimmick, an affront. She considered carrying a machete the way Ricardo did on Halloween. She would wave it in the air when any of them spit at her.

Ricardo lived below her, with Frankie and his grandmother, who was Ricardo's mother, and the other kids, in the crowded Lopez apartment. There were many children. The children had children. Elizabeth came to appreciate the continuity. She saw life going on, stunted and obstructed as it usually was, but she could understand generations because of the Lopezes. They were people who would survive almost anything.

Ricardo had been away a long time, since before Elizabeth and Roy's time, that's what Frankie told her, Ricardo was away, until Frankie told her that Ricardo had been in jail, for drugs. Now he was back, on the block. He carried a machete on Halloween. He stood in front of the laundromat, across the street, holding the machete down the side of his leg. His mother stood next to him, and inside the laundromat Frankie was helping people with their wash. Ricardo was a Puerto Rican nationalist. The Puerto Rican flag hung from their fire escape all year long.

Elizabeth saw the machete. Ricardo held it tight against the side of his body. It shimmered along the leg of his black sweatpants. He had sweat on his forehead. Ricardo explained that gangs were going up and down the streets, with razors, slashing people. For no reason. He was going to get them if they tried anything here. He glared and looked up the block. She knew he wouldn't kill her, he'd protect her. She lived in his building, she was in his territory, and he liked her. She'd let him patronize her, be macho for her as much as he wanted. She'd like to see him slice off one of the crusties' heads.

There are three people—a priest, a rabbi, and a lawyer—standing outside a school. It's on fire, burning down. Children at the window screaming, crying. The Rabbi goes, Oh my God, oh my god. . . . The children, the poor children. The lawyer says, Oh, fuck the children. The priest says, You think we can?

That night when Ernest and Elizabeth walked to the Pick Me Up the crusties were lying on the sidewalk. One of them spit. His spit didn't hit her. That was lucky. Elizabeth was ready to hit him. She wanted to ask the most disgusting crustie, Do you have sex together? How? But she and Ernest had to talk about the tenant situation and their letter.

Ernest hadn't gotten any roles lately. He read a lot of the books in the bookstore where he worked. They discussed, with an intensity that astonished Elizabeth, the letter to the landlord. Elizabeth didn't want the letter to be too meek or too hawkish. She wanted the right tone. When you demand to be treated fairly, you must appear to be just, right but not righteous, and, especially, Elizabeth knew, you must appear to be above suspicion mentally. The last thing she wanted the City to think was that she and Ernest were irrational, that they didn't have a reasonable leg to stand on.

The very next night Ernest came over. He sat next to her on a chair. She sat at her desk, at her laptop. Roy sat in the kitchen, reading. She typed the letter. They considered everything in it, every detail.

To the City,
*xxx and xxy are TWO SEPARATE buildings. . . .[they both wanted capital letters]. No hallway renovation was done in our building; in fact there*

71

is NO downstairs hallway at all [a surprising turn; good to be entertaining].
. . . Tenants of our building do not benefit from the hallway work done on the
building next door—they are ENTIRELY separate buildings [making the point
another way]. . . . Landlord has been belligerent with tenant, who complained of
inadequate hall maintenance. [The tenant was Elizabeth. Ernest urged, Go on,
put that in. Elizabeth happily typed it in.]. . . . Entry to xxx can be made without
key, merely by pushing door open. (Tenant complains of strange man sleeping in
hallway 4/93.) [Ernest was on the top floor. Homeless people slept and shit at his
door.]. . . . Tenants feel it is unfair for building to have been neglected for so long
and then landlord receives increase for fixing it. [Absolutely, they said in unison.]

Elizabeth was especially content with the summary.

The landlord has misrepresented its claims on both xxx and xxy . . . hallway
repairs ACTUALLY done were feeble. [Feeble? Elizabeth asked Ernest. That's
good, he said. His brow furrowed. He repeated the word. FEEBLE. Perfect, be
said.] Number of rooms in xxx and xxy is exaggerated. [The use of exaggerated
was a convincing understatement.] Cleanliness of xxx in particular is poor. The
building is not SAFE. Landlord has received MANY complaints.

Late at night, beyond sleep, she read over and corrected the
words she'd typed. She grew more outraged at the landlord's bold-
faced lies. Her aggravated blood made her face and body blush.
Indignation charged through her. The letter was a romance novel to
her. Roy told her not to believe everything she read. He reminded
her that she wasn't going to do anything about the landlord's letter
until Ernest came along. Elizabeth hung her head in shame. Then she
laughed until she cried.

Ernest mailed the fourteen-page, thoroughly documented letter to the appropriate City agency. With the Polaroids, with maps, with drawings of windows, with measurements, with tenant letters and testimonies, with the valuable petition. Ernest had done his work, Elizabeth had done hers too. Ernest and Elizabeth nailed the landlord in a scandal of lies. They also mailed a letter to the landlord, telling the landlord they had filed with the City. The landlord was on notice.

Then Elizabeth and Ernest rested their case. They waited. They waited for months.

A man went to his psychiatrist and said, Doctor, I don't know what's wrong with me. I'm a tepee, I'm a wigwam, I'm a tepee, I'm a wigwam, I'm a tepee, I'm a wigwam. The psychiatrist said, Relax, you're two tents.

The landlord backed down. The landlord was forced to back down. Each tenant received a letter saying that the increase wouldn't go into effect. The landlord didn't say why, the landlord didn't admit to having been challenged by the tenants. The landlord in fact pretended it was out of concern, some human tenderness on its part, that it had decided to rescind the rent hike. For the time being.

It was an empty victory. No one but her, Ernest, Roy, and Herbert, the deaf guy, noticed. No one mentioned it or seemed to care. Everyone went on living their own little lives. The rent for the apartments they lived in, however miserably, hadn't been raised. She didn't know why it mattered, why she and Ernest had even bothered.

After their blank victory, Ernest and Elizabeth rarely saw

each other. Sometimes she heard him upstairs, walking around or exercising.

Now Elizabeth thought she saw Jeanine go into a doorway several buildings down the block. Elizabeth had to turn her head severely to the right to see that far down the block.

It was Jeanine.

Jeanine prostituted for drugs sometimes, for rent other times. She was a runner for a dealer on the corner. She and Elizabeth had known each other a while. Jeanine came over to her, on the corner, when it was cool, when the corner wasn't busy, and they'd talk. The dealers and runners were a stable crew, and though they were busted in sweeps once in a while they always came back, and were part of the neighborhood. They knew Elizabeth and she knew them, and they didn't hassle each other. When a fight erupted over turf, she made sure not to be there.

It was Jeanine.

Jeanine had been the girlfriend of one of the Lopezes, Jorge. She was the mother of their three children. Elizabeth bought the first baby a present. Jeanine said it was the only one the baby received.

Jorge and Jeanine sat on the stoop in front of the building holding the infant, and then they didn't because it was taken away by the City. Jeanine explained that they had to go to the agency to see it. The agency controlled chunks of Jeanine's and Jorge's lives, because they'd had a child and they themselves were legally children and on drugs. Jeanine said she was trying to stay straight.

Jeanine became pregnant again. Then this child was taken away from her, and Jorge and she started getting high again. Then Jorge got deeper into shit, and into more trouble, and they both went down, down the well together, and the third baby was taken away. All the kids were placed in foster care. Then Jeanine went to prison. The Lopezes said Jorge was in Puerto Rico. Jorge was in jail. He and Jeanine were over.

If Jeanine wasn't on the street, dealing, if she wasn't in jail upstate, she lived at her mother's.

Looking out the window, Elizabeth remembered the afternoon Jeanine came over and slept on her bed. She remembered it as if it were yesterday. Roy was at work. Jeanine'd been up all night. Her mother wouldn't let her into their apartment.

—Until I was about five, we all lived together. It was, like, happy. My mother had four girls and four boys. My mother separated from my father, she became a drunk, started using drugs, heroin, and when they got back together, he molested me, and he ended up molesting my little brother and sister. I think he molested my other brother too, but I'm not sure. They don't speak on it. It caused problems between my mother and me. She blamed me for it. She was in denial for a long time. It happened to my little brother and sister when I went to jail the first time. My father was a really messed-up guy. He used to be a numbers man. He took money and disappeared. Then she had another boyfriend, but she's always insecure about me and her men, like maybe they want me, or I want them. I'm like, please, these old men, get out of my face.

Elizabeth was thinking about how she'd do in jail.

—It's all how the mind handles it, if they break your spirit. I guess it's tough because people tell you when to eat, when to sleep, when to shit. And they do any little thing to provoke you to get into trouble to lock you in solitary, make it hard for you to get out. 'Cause if you're in the city, you can do up to a year, and you have a day to go home; but if you're upstate, they can keep you from going home, they can hold you there. You're dead. You hear from the outside world, but their life goes on without you, so it's like you don't exist. I didn't have a hard time. That's probably why I don't fear going back. But I don't want to go back. Some people go in with this attitude, they try to be too tough, and people beat them up. A lot of people from this neighborhood go. A lot of people have been in jail before—the more times you go, the more people you know. It's like you're a fixture. It would be very hard for middle-class people, people like you. My mother'd been incarcerated before I was ever born.

Jeanine slept for a while. Then she woke up and they had coffee at the rectangular table in the kitchen.

—Do you hate your mother?

—No, I love the old goat. She's a pain in the ass. I want to hurt her sometimes. We've had fights.

—If you don't buy her drugs.

—She has a fit. You pay to stay home, you pay to stay somewhere else. I gotta give her drugs, because I know she has a fit. She's had a hard time. My mother's father raised them. Her mother abused them from when she was little. My mother was in the hospital for three years because she was getting beaten very badly. Then they grew up in homes, because they took them away from her father because back then it was a man with little girls. Then my mother came back home, and she was with my father since she was thirteen years old. My father was older, twenty-six, she was like thirteen or something. Hello. She should have realized then the man had a problem.

Elizabeth nodded sympathetically.

—Jorge used to beat me. First of all, he had an inferiority complex. I had to teach him how to read. The home setting was not happy. Very disturbed. He had the heroin habit. His sister died from AIDS, from shooting up.

Emilia's funeral. Jeanine couldn't handle it, too heavy.

—Jorge killed somebody during a robbery. They're not too kind with you taking somebody's life to deprive them of their property. If you kill somebody in a crime of passion or self-defense, it's one thing; but if you kill someone to take their property from them, it's worse. Jorge's crazy. The heroin, man. When he was so sick he didn't want to hear nothing, and he had attitude, and he wanted to beat everybody up, and blamed the world cause he was sick. When he was straight he didn't want to be bothered; he wanted to enjoy his high. There was no in between. He became crazy shooting up towards the end. He didn't cry for anything. He cried when my kids were taken. But this guy didn't cry for nothing, except one day his fucking set of works got clogged, and he cried like a baby. That's when I really started staying away from the house. It gets to the point where I'm like numb, I really am.

Elizabeth wondered how Jeanine protected herself on the corner.

—The customers are more dangerous, because you don't know them. Though I got my leg broken out there, when the boss guy came out with a bat because somebody said someone was selling something besides his merchandise. We don't harm customers, in fact, people in the neighborhood say they feel safer coming home because they know we're standing there. I'll walk down a drug block before I'll walk down a deserted block. People are not likely to try and drop someone on a block where there's drug dealers, because they're afraid. I'm not afraid of my colleagues, I'm more afraid of my customers, because I've been raped by customers. One girl was chopped up in pieces, we don't know who did it. You get some weird customers, they come out and like they're mixing. These are people who don't get high on a daily basis. Some do—they're real cool. Some people that don't, they're mixing alcohol or coke, heroin and pills and everything all at one time. They're not stable. plus whatever problems drove them to get high. They want to take you somewhere. It's bad to get in a car, I used to, but I had an incident. Sometimes I have customers, when I see them really messed up I don't want to sell to them. They're more dangerous to us than anyone. Most of the regular cops don't bother you. Sometimes they have nights when they want you off the corner, they come by, slow down and say, Take a walk. There's this older black guy we call Batman. He beats up the guys. He just gets out of the car and beats them up. He won't even take them to jail. Just beats the shit out of them.

Batman the cartoon or because he uses a bat?

—He's a black man. I'm black myself, but this guy's blacker than my shit. He's even got this gold ring that has this Batman picture. His partner is six foot seven—they call him Robin. He's terrible. They're terrible. But they won't beat up the girls, There aren't that many girls out there, but they won't really beat us up. Which makes them angry, they get more angry at us because they can't really search us. But there are more female cops now, before you never saw them. This younger guy, he used to always want to talk to you, offer you help. If he arrested you, it would be because he felt like you needed a break. There used to be two sisters down the block. They were saving their money to go to school, so the cops wouldn't arrest them.

Jeanine ate a sandwich. Elizabeth told her about wanting to murder someone, anyone, when she couldn't sleep. Jeanine laughed at her.

—Some nights are really messed up. It gets bad out there. A lot of people are high. A lot of people learn to get for themselves. We're middlemen, we're going to purchase it from a certain place. They don't want to commit a felony themselves. They might get beaten or they might get hurt, so they're willing to pay us double the price to get it for them. But a lot of customers are getting bold and they're going themselves. Some people got cleaned up. Once you could make a thousand dollars just out there a night; these days if it's a hundred bucks you're lucky. Coke's played out.

Jeanine drank some more coffee. She had a shower. She came out wrapped in a towel.

—All the guys I have used to be cops. Isn't that weird? All the cops come over to me. It's weird. They like me, they're trying to get me off the block, but they end up giving me money to buy drugs. Cops come and buy drugs, not from here, from elsewhere. From other precincts, whatever. The guy I've been seeing for a while, he's married, and he wanted me to stay stuck in the house, and it was just not a healthy situation. If she's here, I wouldn't see him for three or four days in a row, then I won't see him for two weeks. A really uncomfortable situation, and I become very obsessed with him, and I didn't think that was cool. Somebody else's man. He's alright, he used to be a cop. He's a very nice guy. Some no-good man— that's my worst addiction. I'm addicted to no-good men. Or being addicted to anything, you know what I'm saying? Your body has to keep up with your mind. I'll run to avoid sitting and thinking and facing reality. A lot of people in the neighborhood speak to me, want to help me, say I'm nice. I don't belong out there. I tell them, I don't know. It's my lifestyle now.

Elizabeth said it was a job, she saw her working on the corner almost every day.

—My job? Yeah, it's my job. True. And before, there used to be a lot of money. The flow was nonstop. A lot of people got clean. A lot of customers went bankrupt. Lost their jobs. A lot of customers had to stop to maintain their lives. A lot of men, their wives don't know what they're doing, and they screw up and their wives find out. There's women too, but it's usually couples if there's a woman involved, or like a lot of teenagers. I won't serve to teenagers, but there's college kids buying weed and stuff, then you see a lot of girls. A lot of people are smart enough to give it up instead of giving up their lives. Or it's too expensive. Sign of the times.

Jeanine looked at the clock on the kitchen wall. She had to make her group therapy session. She dressed, brushed her hair and put on orange lipstick.

—The last two months with my leg broken I couldn't report, and I couldn't get any outpatient therapy. It wasn't my fault. You go there, a group meeting, which is so stupid. I can't understand why parole and probation want to send you somewhere where you sit around and hear stories about drugs. Even in jail. I go to jail and sit in these little encounter groups, and every time I come out the drug I try is different from the one I used before. Because I heard about it in some meeting. They make you go and by the time you're finished with these meetings you want to get high. It's like really ridiculous. I don't want to go back. I won't sell to someone unless I know them. So many undercovers, you can't even tell who they are. I'm still on parole. They can lie on you, just 'cause you have a record, you can go to jail forever, you know? You gotta be real careful out there.

It was Jeanine in the doorway. She was gobbling some guy's dick for the price of a rock.

—You gotta be real careful out there.

Elizabeth wondered if Ernest was awake, lying in bed, or at the window above hers. Maybe he was naked, at his window. Maybe he was watching Jeanine. Maybe he was summer hot or excited. Jeanine in the doorway. Elizabeth liked sex, she liked watching sex.

Maybe Ernest could sleep through noise. Sleep through anything. Like Roy. Lights on in two more apartments. Babies crying. Dogs barking. One horrific scream. Then silence.

Now a door opened across the street.

The young super from the building on the other side of the street walked out his front door. Onto the street. He glanced from east to west. He played the role of an important man expecting someone or something. He couldn't have expected to catch the morons. They were gone. He shuffled in an aggravated way to the overturned garbage cans. He saw the damage. He cursed loudly. His arms flapped up and down, jerking out from his body. He checked his car. It was OK. The one next to his was dented. He didn't react. The garbage-can throwers weren't on the church steps. The young super took his time. He was a creep.

There's a restaurant on the moon.
Yeah?
Great food, no atmosphere.

Why don't cannibals eat clowns?
They taste funny.

When the young super first took over the building across the street, he worked on his car every day. sometimes he worked on it early, five A.M., six A.M. He'd rev it up and turn the engine over. Over and over. Elizabeth became aware of him. He woke her up. she'd run to the window, stare out, and see him at dawn looking at his coughing car. Maybe his hands would be tinkering with the car's insides. Dawn was just another ruined night. Sometimes she'd open the window and shout, Stop it, stop it. Please. He never heard. He couldn't hear over his engine. The noise went on and on. Furious like churlish garbagetrucks, incessant like boisterous oil trucks fueling boilers in basements.

The young super was revving his engine again. No one else was alive to him. Elizabeth lay there with her eyes open. The noise grew louder. It always did. She started to inch out of bed. To slide to the end of the bed. Her toenails were hard. She gouged Roy on his calf.

—What are you doing? Roy asked.

—I'm not telling you, Elizabeth said.

—Where are you going?

—I'm going for a walk.

—In the middle of the night.

—It's dawn.

—Get back in bed.

—I can't sleep.

—Get back here, Lizard. Go to sleep.

—I can't. He's revving his engine again.

—He's got a right to work on his car.

—This is a residential area.

—What are you going to do?

—Tell him to stop.

—You're going to get killed.

—OK.

—Don't do anything, don't be a jerk.

She might have to die to sleep. She laughed out loud. It sounded hollow in the apartment. She put on her robe and Japanese canvas shoes. Roy pulled the blanket over his head. His back was to her. He'd already accepted her death. Maybe she was as good as dead.

Roy didn't want Elizabeth at an open window in the middle of the night, or at dawn, he didn't want her getting involved, staring down or checking out a commotion on the street, especially a fight between drugged-out, warring guys or between a man and a woman, over sex, money, or drugs. He didn't want her sticking her head out the window. He told her about a couple of newlyweds who were on a train, on their honeymoon. They were going to the country. The bridegroom stuck his head out of the window of the train. A pole or something jutting out decapitated him, sliced his head right off. Then he fell back into the compartment, headless. And his bride went mad.

Elizabeth didn't think that would happen to her. An illegal windowbox could drop from the windowsill above and crush her head, but even then there wouldn't be enough speed or thrust for her head to be chopped off. Her skull could be flattened to a bloody pulp, but her head wouldn't be sliced off like a chunk of fat white meat.

Roy returned to Roy's world.

Elizabeth opened her door and walked down the stairs. The halls were even bleaker in the middle of the night. Dawn. Farmers woke like this every morning, at the break of day, milked cows, sloshed around in the heat or cold, fed pigs who were more intelligent than they were, grew wrinkled and weather-beaten, and their wives cooked heartbreaking breakfasts, shriveled under the sun, nursed belligerent youngsters or died in childbirth. Everyone's a hero. Elizabeth giggled then stifled herself. There were cigarette butts on the stairs and floors, tissues, candy wrappers, an empty paper bag. Nothing big. No vomit or blood or needles. Only some Phillies Blunt tobacco the kids mixed with marijuana. Grass. Weed. Tree.

Elizabeth marched stiffly across the street to the super at his car. She was in her robe, outside, on the street. She knew she looked ridiculous. People do when they act on principle. Like clowns in the circus. She'd only been to one circus. It was a crazy theater, the rings, the animals, the red-lipped clowns hanging from ropes. The audience fears the worst and waits for it. She counted herself a silent, anonymous member of Clowns for Progress. The group plastered its posters around the neighborhood.

Elizabeth stood beside the super until he decided to notice her. She was closer than she'd ever been to him. It was a grotesque intimacy. When he noticed her, she spoke as calmly as she could.

—You may not realize it, but some people are still trying to sleep. Maybe even until eight or nine this morning. Do you realize how loud your engine is? And do you know that it's against the law? It's noise pollution. Disturbing the peace. I could call the cops. I won't, but I could. I can't sleep. I can't stand it anymore. Don't you ever think about anyone else?

She stood there. She had finished her speech. She waited beside him, in her robe. He stared at her. His answer was silent revulsion. His disgust should have been reserved for battle, when a soldier calls up the desire to destroy from a vat of villainous mixed emotions. Pleasure, revulsion, and fear animate the killing machine. Soldiers are allowed legal murder.

The young super, smartly dressed but his nose streaked with grease, had no understanding of quiet in the morning. No respect for other people who needed their sleep. Elizabeth could see that. She enlivened his killing machine. He and she stood their ground. Her ground felt puny and groundless. They were locked in a barbaric embrace. It was public. They could be watched by anyone. Someone might be videotaping them for a stupid TV show. She was candid and conspicuous. The young super despised her. His rage shaped and reshaped his face. She would've slapped him if she thought he wouldn't murder her. She wanted to wipe the expression off his face. Murder was too good for him. That's what her mother would say. He didn't raise a hand, and the law held Elizabeth's hand. They were both held in check. An abyss yawned, wide and filthy, like a domestic Persian Gulf. She hated her own voice which repeated:

—Don't you understand that there are other people on the block? Don't you understand? People need to sleep. There are other people on the block.

The young super's face had hardened into furious incomprehension. Then he turned away from her, turned his back to her, returned to his car's engine, ignored her existence, and she walked back across the street to her building, walked back up the filthy stairs, went back to her position at the window. Elizabeth wondered who, if anyone, had witnessed the event. A friend or an enemy. Roy slept through it.

Now one of the dogwalkers marched out. He was usually the first on the block. He carried a single paper towel. He had a little dog. Most carried newspapers or plastic bags. Roy picked up newspaper from the street and used it for Fatboy, their dog. His dog. Dogwalkers walked their dogs and waited until the dog took a shit and then they scooped it up. They threw it into garbage cans. Most of them did this flawlessly. Gracefully. They'd had practice. There were a variety of methods. Newspaper under their dogs' asses. The dogs were trained to do it on the paper. Plastic bag on the hand like a glove. Owner grabs the shit and like a surgeon removes the glove with the shit and drops it into the garbage can. Each one had a technique, different for different dogs. The pooper scooper law was enacted under Mayor Koch. It was his legacy to the city, what he'd be remembered for, New Yorkers picking up dog shit. Along with an impartial judicial review board and handing over the city, opening it up like a high-class brothel, to the real estate clowns. That was years ago.

Now she wouldn't confront the young super, or anyone, alone on the street. Crime was down, but on what basis do they figure those stats, and even if there were fewer murders, she still wouldn't take the chance. People were more apathetic, exhausted, they were back on heroin, off crack, it didn't matter, it could change, and statistics lie any way you want them to, and if you're lying in the street, blood flowing from a wound in your head or stomach, because one of the fewer murders has been attempted, or achieved, it's you lying on the street, it's your bloody body, lifeless or hurt, and it doesn't matter what the stats are.

Elizabeth didn't have that many chances. No one did.

Now she considered the enduring consequences of announcing her grievances to her neighbors. Elizabeth had been ignorant of the fact that Hector the super had befriended the young super. His name was Ahmed, she didn't know which Middle Eastern country he was from, and Hector was Ahmed's block mentor. She hadn't known that. After Hector heard about what she did, he was barely civil to her.

Roy told Elizabeth she had to learn to accept the unacceptable.

She tried and slipped and told the woman on the first floor, Diane, that the woman on the top floor bothered her. The top floor woman screamed at her boyfriend's child from early morning on, and when she was high on coke, ran out in the night, forgot her keys and screamed for her mate to throw her a key, to let her in. He'd punish her, want to teach her a lesson. He'd be disgusted. He'd want out. He'd pretend not to hear the wailing, subhuman shrieks everyone else heard. Finally he'd give in, let her in. She'd whimper all the way up the stairs. Past Elizabeth's door. Then they'd fuck probably. Elizabeth complained to the woman on the first floor about how the craziness was driving her crazy. The first-floor woman said she was friends with the top-floor woman.

—Do you want me to talk with her? she asked.

—No, no, please, I'll handle it, Elizabeth said.

Elizabeth retreated. She had to be more careful. Roy thought she was a jerk. She had to let people know what she felt or thought. He told her she was chronicling her life. He'd watched a TV news special about women talking on the telephone. It said they were chronicling their lives.

The young super never looked at her on the street. He wouldn't help her if someone was trying to cut her, cap her, molest her. He was an enemy on the block. He wouldn't lift a finger to save her life. In the city, you can have enemies and never see them. It's urbane, humane. But if you have enemies on your block, you can't count on them. Not even in a lethal situation. They might applaud the bad guys or be apathetic bystanders, even grandstanders. Yeah, they could say later grinning, yeah, I saw him take that bitch and grab her head and slam it against the wall . . .

Elizabeth daydreamed that the young super Ahmed would come to her aid. Even though he hated her, he'd help her. He'd overcome his hatred and save her life. They'd forget their enmity, they'd forget the past. They'd become friends, and there would be one less problem in her little world. It was a fairy tale. It was like a dream when an ex-friend appeared and said, I love you. Or something. Elizabeth cried over spilt milk, the irreconcilable.

But Ahmed, wherever he came from, hated her. He still hated her. He would always hate her. He still lived on her block. He would always live on her block. He had a family now. The young super had a wife. They had one or two babies. Some nasty people are loved by apparently nice people. The young super's wife usually had a benign expression on her face. Elizabeth watched her get into and out of the young super's new car. Elizabeth decided he slapped her around. The wife's placid expression masked fear. Her abjection was as great as the enmity between Elizabeth and the young super. But Elizabeth couldn't ask him, Have you stopped beating your wife? He wouldn't get the joke.

They found a woman on Fourteenth Street in a bathtub full of milk.
They did?
With a banana jammed up her ass.
You're kidding.
The cops are looking for a cereal killer.

Why are there so few black serial killers?
Why?
No ambition.

Elizabeth hated the country. Small-town life was jail. Country people huddled together like sheep near one-movie towns, without bookstores or restaurants. They drove to abysmal malls for action. They planted huge antennae and satellite dishes on their lawns to hook themselves up to the world, which they didn't want any part of. They lived in nature, didn't see it, didn't care about it. They knew everything about each other. They saw each other every day and passed the time: Looks like Sally isn't getting out much anymore.

It was on TV. Elizabeth watched TV. She liked windows. TV's cranky hermits and serial killers were at the dark heart of the country's dark side. They were the children taught to distrust anyone not like them, children of incest, thin-blooded, with dead, flat eyes, they were genetic threats. They fucked harnessed animals who kicked them in the head. Hermits passed bleak nights knitting shrouds, cleaning their shotguns, or fuming about grievances long past. Hermits plotted. Serial killers thrived and grew bloodthirsty for company in isolated outposts. The city's a cold place, the story goes. But in the country, your barn burns down, they raise a new one with you, you get a smile and a howdy in the country.

There was no anonymity for hate, love, or lust in the country. Elizabeth could've fucked the super as easily as killed him.

The young super hadn't revved his engine that early in the morning for a long time. Elizabeth didn't know if it was because of her. She'd spelled it out to him that she could call the cops and have him arrested for disturbing the peace, which she didn't, but it may have made an impression on him. It may have made no impression on him. If he hadn't cared about waking other people, hadn't thought it was wrong, he wouldn't have cared about disturbing the peace.

Everybody understood, I'll call the cops. Everyone on the block understood that.

Maybe he was an illegal immigrant, hiding, living in fear. If she threatened him now after his years in New York—maybe back then he'd just arrived and was adjusting to America, was still peaceful, even content to be here, if he was, maybe he'd escaped a worse situation. Now he'd probably hit her with a car wrench or throw her under his car, grab the jack and let the car drop on her, killing her, not instantly, slowly. Painfully. It could be made to seem like an accident unless people were around to witness it or people knew they'd had an incident in the past. That's why it's necessary to tell people about fights you have with crazy people. Later the crazy person might come after you, and if no one knew there was a motive, your life could be ended and the cops would never find your killer. Never bring him to justice. Elizabeth couldn't convince Roy about the necessity of communicating to other people the malevolent acts of crazy people. Roy didn't make small talk.

The young super might grab his wrench and strike violently at her skull, knocking out enough brain cells to alter her functioning. She'd be mentally disabled. Or, if the car landed on her legs, maybe she wouldn't die, she'd only be crippled for life. That would be worse than death. She'd have to move out of her rent-stabilized apartment on the fifth floor. It was a walk-up.

Elizabeth held her vulnerable head in her hands. She rocked.

She knew about several people's failed suicide attempts. They were in wheelchairs or using canes. Everyone hated them for what they'd done to themselves. There's no sympathy for failure and no sympathy for failed suicides who end up crippled. Failure doesn't negate failure. Elizabeth ended a friendship with someone who tried to kill himself. It was cruel, it was inexplicable. Cruelty and kindness are. Elizabeth had the sense that the guy would hurt someone else, her, because you hurt the ones you love, who are within reach, because he failed at killing himself.

Another light went on. A first-floor window. Then a fourth-floor window. Maybe other supers were waking up, readying themselves to meet and greet the day. There'd be garbage on the streets. They knew that. They were prepared for that.

A woman super, Polish or Ukrainian, created a racket every other day, fixing her garbage cans. She was pretty old, so she couldn't lift them. She'd drag them from one part of the sidewalk to another, drag drag drag, clank clank clank. Elizabeth never called the cops or yelled out the window even though the woman woke her. The old Polish woman did her job, she kept her part of the sidewalk clean. She placed the covers on the garbage cans. She wasn't Hector.

It was too early for the old Polish super in her weather-beaten brown coat, flannel nightgown, funny plastic shoes, and babushka. Summer or winter. A jogger trotted by. Elizabeth ignored joggers. Especially when they spun their heels at red lights and jogged in place beside her, waiting for the light to change. They panted and sweated and gulped water from plastic bottles. She expected them to drop dead next to her.

If Elizabeth became crippled and ugly, no one would feel sorry for her, even though it wasn't her fault, and she wasn't trying to commit suicide, although some people would say, Living in that neighborhood is suicide, what'd she expect? Crippled, she'd have to move. She wouldn't be able to walk up or down four flights of stairs, and no one would be able to carry her. Not even Roy. He'd probably leave her. She wouldn't be able to exercise. She'd become enormously fat. She'd wallow in her weight, her rolls of fat. It would be her only reward. Maybe she'd need an oversized wheelchair. She wondered if they were available or if you had to have them custom made. That would cost a fortune. She had no place to keep it.

She didn't want to move. She didn't want to be crippled. The man next door was crippled. He had a ground-floor apartment. He'd never move. He couldn't roll into Kim's Video Store because it wasn't wheelchair friendly. The wheelchair man told her that. She thought of speaking to the owner. He'd begun as a dry cleaner and branched into video stores. He probably never thought about wheelchair access.

She dreaded apartment hunting, standing in the center of an empty apartment with a rent she couldn't afford, even though she'd rather die than live in it. It was grotesque, being enclosed by four shabby walls, and not being able to afford it, or even finding yourself considering renting it. It was tenement despair. What you really wanted was inaccessible. With or without a wheelchair. Pathetic. It made her want a house that wasn't for rent, that couldn't be taken from her, anywhere, a house anywhere except in the country. She knew some people who liked to apartment hunt. It was inconceivable. It's what makes horse racing. No one she knew followed the races.

—Even a journey of a thousand miles begins with the following cancellations, Roy said once.

Elizabeth's murderous impulses were ordinary, that's what made them dangerous. She'd never do time, like Jeanine, who expected it, like middle-class kids expect to go to college. Elizabeth wouldn't do time, unless life became more unpredictable than it had been. It could happen in time. Time could do it to her, do her, anything could happen.

The super who hated her walked back into his apartment building.

She even hated the way he walked. It was an insolent, arrogant swagger, almost indecent. He disappeared into his pitiful, creepy world, hidden in his apartment building. His building was next to the laundromat.

The laundromat was one of the centers on the block. She could watch the dryers from her window. She and Roy knew when to do the laundry. From their windows they could see how many dryers were empty. They could also check when their dryer had stopped spinning.

It's impossible to be on both sides of the window simultaneously. Windows were paradoxical. She was vulnerable with them, vulnerable without them. She had to be wary of attack, but she had to be open. She was not an eyeless mollusk in a cave, she needed air and light. At the window, she made an effort to think about how she was seen and if she was being seen. She was like a window, she thought, sometimes transparent, usually paradoxical, and always open to tragicomic views of life.

She liked watching people do their laundry, but she didn't like doing it. Roy did the laundry more than she did. It didn't bother him. Occasionally she found herself enjoying it. She recognized that the pleasure might be the onset of a disease, wholesomeness. Clothes just became dirty again, dirtier, so the activity was endless and unimportant. People washed and dried their clothes in moments of great, incommensurable despair. For many, it was their finest hour.

It depended on your point of view. views were always a problem. Elizabeth didn't own her view. A builder could buy air rights to the building across the street and destroy what she saw, steal her light.

Finally Jeanine finished the guy off. They left the doorway. Maybe he was a cop.

—All the guys I have used to be cops. Isn't that weird? Some no-good man-that's my worst addiction. I'm addicted to no-good men.

The sun was orange and furious. It was engorged, insensible. There was nothing Elizabeth could do about Jeanine, the elusiveness of sleep, or the stagnant effects of memory. sleep wouldn't absolve her anyway. It wasn't her friend. Who was a friend. Friends and enemies come and go. They're turncoats, reversible. She hated reversible coats. She didn't see the point.

Elizabeth turned herself inside out and threw herself into reverse, into regret, remorse, and the puny unspeakable.

You wonder why as you sit and nurse old wounds and new sores you wonder why I vanished that night, you were inside yourself, rotting like dead meat, your paranoid stories poisoned me, it's my fault I listened, I'm tired of doing that, even so I love our past, isn't that funny, but I can't be next to it, you don't hear yourself, you have no idea.

She wouldn't have friends or enemies for long because life was mercilessly and mercifully short. Her days were numbered. Her nights didn't count. She had to put up with noise. Noise was the voice of the people. Raucous laughter erupted from somewhere. Then a bloodcurdling scream and more bloodstopping laughter.

Hector was the super of her building. He couldn't take care of it. He spoiled it, he dirtied it. His very existence negated what he was paid to do. She had to accept that. The problem isn't always plain incompetence and poor administration. It must have to do with why people take the jobs they do, even if they think they don't want to do them. They take them because they can't do them. Maybe they hate what they're doing. Not being able to do it, constitutionally, is another thing. Working a job that attacks your worst habit occurs all the time. It's not an accident. People who don't understand mental illness and who are punitive, people with a little money, moderately well-off people, think neuroses are a luxury. They blather on about poor people, how the poor don't have time to be neurotic. It only demonstrates the narrow-mindedness of the nonpoor. If they're out of work, which makes them poor and crazy, the poor have all the time in the world to be neurotic.

Rich people were blocked. Poor people were blocked. They blocked other people. She saw them. They set up obstacles for themselves, for her and everyone else. It was amazing she could walk down the block.

Elizabeth pictured a listing in the employment section of the *Times*:

### HELP WANTED

Someone who would never have considered it, because it's menial work, someone who finds pleasure in fixing and washing things, think about this: You might consider becoming a super. If anxious about maintenance, you'd do the job well, if worried about spots and grime, you might be the one. You could achieve success in an underestimated field. Any tenant can attest to how important a super is.

It's a small world, someone said to Jackie Curtis.
Not if you have to clean it, Jackie Curtis answered.

Her day was about to eclipse her night.

Some will never be clean enough, some can't clean, some don't want to, some are doomed, some want others to do it for them, some hate putting their hands in hot water. Some love filth and shit and dirt, some roll in it. Not that many, but some. Hector is one. But some people love cleaning so much, they can hardly admit it. Their hands become raw and dry and they keep their hands in steaming water and they soak off life's filth, and they make themselves smell good and they let nothing collect on their tables or on the floor. They're happy. They're clean. They think they're safe. They've kept life's grime off them. It's a constant battle. They're private sanitation workers. Cleanliness is next to anything. It's just itself. It becomes its opposite, a viler identical twin.

Maybe Hector understood this and didn't even try. He collected instead. If it can't be cleaned, it can be collected.

Anyone can collect anything, any dumb trinket is collectible. Put enough of them together and you'll get money for the collection. Some other moron will give you money because you collected hotel matchbooks, coasters, or autographs from movie stars who'd spit on you if they could. Empty feelings were temporarily negated by being smothered and surrounded by thousands of the same kind of thing, mounting and mounted. People start collecting on a whim. It just happened, they say. They just started. They started with one baseball card, porcelain cupid, button, postcard, and then it took over their lives, consumed them. They never know why. They say, I thought I'd get another one, then I wanted another one, and suddenly, I wanted this one, and then I wanted all of them. I had to have the whole set, all of them. The stuff's all around them, in boxes or cartons, or displayed on shelves. It fills their houses and their lives, the irresistible, the harmless. Their impulses are everywhere. The stuff that isn't collectible collects inside them, silently, cunningly.

What she collected kept her from sleeping. Elizabeth shook herself. She didn't want to go under.

Why do WASPs like taking planes?
For the food.

Two men strolled along the street, talking casually. To them everything was cool. They were in love, they were inviolable. On the next corner they could be murdered by a moron. She'd probably be murdered. Her life would come to its pathetic statistical end, and she wouldn't have murdered anyone, wouldn't know the thrill.

Mindless, heartless, she was on the edge. She was close to the bliss of being unconscious, bodiless. She rubbed her eyes.

Frankie came out on the street again. It was time to open the laundromat. Frankie stretched floridly. His long tan arms flew out from his body and reached to the torrid sky. He stretched his legs. He was a dancer, limbering up. He glanced both ways. He wasn't afraid of cars. He took in the street. It was his as much as anybody's. It was his more than anybody's. He took out the key to the laundromat. He unlocked the padlock. He lifted the heavy iron gate on the plate-glass window. He pushed it up and grunted. The heavy gate made a dramatic, yawning sound.

Frankie's presence was a comfort. Frankie was doing what he was supposed to do. Elizabeth's eyes shut. Her head dropped. Her troublesome body relaxed. She slid onto the couch. She slid below the window and disappeared from sight. Frankie entered the laundromat.

The man in the third-floor window closed his blinds. He turned on the light. He dressed. He cursed.

Jeanine was on another couch, at home, coming down. Her mother was screaming at her, Jeanine ignored her.

—You pay to stay home, you pay to stay somewhere else. I gotta give her drugs, because I know she has a fit. She's had a hard time. My mother's father raised them. Her mother abused them from when she was little. My mother was in the hospital for three years because she was getting beaten very badly. Then they grew up in homes, because they took them away from her father because back then it was a man with little girls. Then my mother came back home, and she was with my father since she was thirteen years old. My father was older, twenty-six, she was like thirteen or something. Hello. She should have realized then the man had a problem.

Elizabeth couldn't help herself. She tucked the street, the endless night, away, into her, she couldn't keep her eyes open, and when she couldn't see what was going on, all the details, the sidewalk antics, when everything was crushed, broken up, and shoveled into the unruliness called her, exceeding her, all more and less than her, then sleep found her, against her will.

Now Elizabeth didn't exist to herself. She wasn't anywhere.

A circus tent fell down, they were trapped, rabid dogs were roaming, cars overturned, bridges down, wolves with blood on their mouths grimaced, some people escaped, they carried everything on their backs, there were cresting waves and falling screams, a vast territory with decrepit buildings, and something was moving very fast, she was in slow motion.

Her feet were stuck, the boss was not in his office, and her mother was sad, she was unable to walk, and small people, dwarfs, made high-pitched yowling noises, they were bedraggled, they were children, and no one had shoes on, her mother was wasting away, dying, she didn't think anyone loved her, she couldn't remember who loved her, she wouldn't ever again know where she was, and Elizabeth, who was old, then young, a teenager, walked unevenly into the movie theater, with her mother, who was frail, she had to be carried to her seat, but she didn't have her ticket, and handed in her shoes which didn't have heels on them, and a black ten-year-old boy with a golden boombox told her a glass bottle had exploded, white hyenas had thrown bottles at him, and the young boy dropped his pants, and there were shards of glass stuck in his ass, he was bleeding, Jeanine was in a doorway, a woman's face appeared in a mirror, she was putting on make-up, her face was a nightmare, she was almost dead, and popcorn was overflowing, and greasy, and her shoes were wrong, and they wouldn't let her in, she pulled a long hair from her coat, and her mother was lost, it would be her turn next, where's the ticket to leave, and there was jostling for a place, ladders collapsing, and noise, but somehow she entered the hall, nothing on the screen, a rope around her waist, she was tugged along, she saw some friends, she was naked suddenly, they asked, what are you doing here, you weren't supposed to be here, you don't live here. . . .

YOU DON'T LIVE HERE
THIS IS A BLOCK PARTY

I have never believed in decorating cells.
—Nelson Mandela, on visiting his former cell at Robben Island

We can only laugh when a joke has come to our help.
—Sigmund Freud

Day and Night

In jail, after she'd murdered the moron, she'd be given one phone call, but only after she'd demanded it. She's gonna lawyer up, a sleek cop would whisper to his partner, the beer-bellied one. Elizabeth didn't know who she'd phone from jail. Roy would think it was a joke. She didn't have a lawyer.

I have the right to remain silent. I have the right to remain single. I have the right to live with someone. I have the right to have a lawyer. I have the right to be sad. I have the right to be stupid. I have the right to be happy when other people are miserable. I have the right to make one telephone call.

Silently Elizabeth gave herself a Miranda warning. You aren't Latin, you aren't going to wiggle your hips for money and wear fruit on your head, you aren't going to turn yourself in to the authorities, even though you are guilty. You will try to destroy the authority within. You are not going to destroy yourself. You will sleep tonight. You are going to quit your job. You are going to tell the fat man off. You are going to tell her to leave you alone.

A car alarm shrieked. The block's wake-up call. Elizabeth flipped over on the couch. She covered her ears with her hands. The alarm screeched, wailed, pulsated, pounded. It demanded and sounded like inevitability. It was torture. There were fewer car alarms. No one paid attention to them because they cried wolf.

The chimes on the church across the street rang dully a few minutes after the hour. 8 A.M.

Her friend used to keep a dozen eggs on his windowsill. When a car alarm went off under his window, especially when he was sick and couldn't sleep, he was always ready to toss eggs. He was tall and had long arms. She never asked him if he hit a car. It was too late to ask. He was dead.

Elizabeth watched the clock tick silently while the car alarm screamed. If one of her foes saw her throw eggs, and that foe owned the car or knew the person whose car it was, if the young super caught her doing it, it could mean trouble for her on the block. She worried about retaliation.

Cops didn't respond to car alarms. She didn't want to think about her dead friend. If she phoned the cops, they'd say they were sending a car. They always said that.

Being alive was its own reward.

Roy was sleeping. So was Fatboy. The alarm clock rang. Unconscious, Roy reached for it. He had a hard time finding it on the floor. He did and shut it off. He was still in Roy's underworld. The car alarm stopped. Heavy feet stomped up the stairs. Doorbells buzzed. Their doorbell. Twice. Rebellious, resigned, Elizabeth grunted and crossed the room. She walked to the broken clothes closet. She was naked. She pulled on her thickest robe. It was the Con Ed man.

The Con Ed man always rang twice. He appeared regularly, once a month. Depending on how eager he was to finish his day, which was the beginning of her day, he woke her at 7, 8, or 9 A.M. She'd put on her robe—he'd be shouting, CON ED CON ED CON ED, buzzing everyone's doorbell—and she'd let him in. He'd beam his flashlight at the meter, he'd punch in the numbers on his blue electronic notepad. Then he'd leave.

Elizabeth wondered how he felt about people in general, what kind of feelings he had about waking everyone, if he did, and how he felt about seeing people in semiconscious states, in their ratty robes, or half-naked, and whether he wanted the job so that he could see people like that. She wondered if his job made him like people more or less.

Elizabeth yelled, OK, wait a second. Her nakedness was covered. She opened the door to Con Ed. It was 8:30 A.M.

—You're late, she said.

He grinned and flashed his light at the meter, punched in the numbers. He appeared sheepish. He bent his head down as he walked out the door. He always lowered his head. He was tall, not as tall as her dead friend. Elizabeth shut the door behind him.

In the hospital her dead friend said to his mother, I'm at peace, then he shut his eyes, went to sleep, and left the world in the early morning of an Independence Day.

The Con Ed man shouted again, CON ED CON ED. Some tenants never opened their doors to him. He probably didn't take it personally, unless he was paranoid. Some tenants figured that the amount of gas and electricity Con Ed estimated was less than what they actually used. Those tenants received an official letter. Con Ed insisted upon reading their meters.

Elizabeth switched on the radio—we'll give you the world, 1010 WINS. She turned the volume low. The radio muttered fitfully. She put a pot of water on the stove. A thread dangled from the gas pipe. It hung there petulantly. It'd been there for half a century. It was there because if there was a gas leak, you could put a match to the thread and then explode.

Roy said she used too much toilet paper. She couldn't accept his leaving the seat up. After years of living with him, she still didn't understand him. She once had a boyfriend who didn't use toilet paper when he pissed, like Roy and other men, but his penis leaked. It left a wet spot on his pants. He had an operation on his penis, performed by his surgeon father. Later, he went to a therapist for a long time. Elizabeth broke up with him three years before Roy came along. She saw him on the street every once in a while. He looked insane.

She switched off the news. She turned on Courtney Love who sang morosely, "I make my bed, I lie in it." She had a right to be miserable. Everyone did.

Elizabeth sat down at the rectangular Formica table in the kitchen. Sunlight or gloom entered through two dirty windows. She wouldn't clean them. She could lose her balance and fall out. The young super would be ecstatic if she cracked her skull open and her brains bled out. He'd be delighted. All her enemies would.

She'd fall onto the backyard patio. There was a backyard, with a tree. A New York tree, a weed. It was unashamed and hardy for a long time. Unabashed, it grew. Now the tree was dying. The landlord didn't tend it. It was suffering from a disease that was probably curable. Gloria was a tree killer. Elizabeth had become attached to the once-sturdy weed. In winter, it shed its leaves and withered. It became skeletal and forlorn. There'd been a weeping willow in front of the house she grew up in. The willow's roots were strong. They made the walkway buckle. Her parents had the willow tree pulled out and thrown away, because it caused trouble. A weeping willow out her bedroom window, a weeping pillow in her bedroom, the tree caused trouble, and she grew up.

A man goes to the pearly gates. St. Peter asks how much he made last year, and he says, $300,000. What'd you do? St. Peter asks. I was a lawyer. Go through, St. Peter says. The next guy comes along, and St. Peter asks him how much he made, and he says, I made $100,000. St. Peter asks, What'd you do? I was a doctor, the guy says. Go through, St. Peter tells him. The next guy arrives, and St. Peter asks him how much he made. I made $7,000, the guy says. St. Peter says, Oh yeah, I think I've heard you play.

Elizabeth was on call for the proofroom today. If one of the obese men was still sick, she'd do some time, a few hours. Yesterday she finished a freelance job—a dictionary, small print-in the room. The room called doing freelance doubledipping. The obese men frowned on it, others just didn't do it, others could care less. As long as you put your freelance away when the pages swished into the basket, you didn't get in trouble with the supervisors.

There's always something that needs to be done around the house, her mother often remarked. It was a reason to hate houses and mothers.

Elizabeth stirred the black coffee in the blue cup. Roy stirred in the bed at the other end of the apartment. She didn't talk to him in the morning. He wasn't available. It wasn't his time.

The air wasn't circulating. It was stolid and stale. When she thought about summer in winter, she didn't remember how dead the air was. People like the change of seasons. They don't remember everything about them.

She had to cut Greta, Regreta, out of her life with surgical precision. It was funny. She'd realized the necessity one night after a rainstorm, when she'd come home soaked and frenetic, and there was another Greta phone call, asking for something and denigrating someone else, the person had taken something from her, used her. Greta regretted everything and complained about the conspiracy of people stealing her ideas, her men, her books, jokes, clothes. Greta was always so calm, reasonable, and compassionate, it'd never occurred to Elizabeth that she schemed or that she was part of Greta's scheme. The revelation came after the thunderstorm.

Elizabeth's wet clothes were lying in a lump on the floor. She kicked them into the bathroom with her bare foot. She listened to Regreta complain and realized, everything she's complaining about she is and does. Elizabeth had to end it.

A friendship ends, and there's no ceremony. There are no tombstones, just marks and wounds that aren't supposed to be there. People want to think that the things they hate are not in them, that what hurts them isn't in them to do, that they're incapable of behavior like that. Almost beyond repair, people did precisely what they complained others did to them. A simple thing was not phoning a friend back and keeping the friend waiting, for days, maybe weeks. Simple sadism. People hated it done to them and did it to other people.

Elizabeth didn't trust herself. She thought primitively, she thought all thought was in a way primitive or basic, there was no purity in thinking, and people were fools to think they could think their way out of their thoughts.

That revelatory spring thunderstorm was huge. The city collapsed under its weight. The tops of roofs crumbled and one or two people were hit on their heads by bricks falling from great heights. They died an absurd death. You finish work and a brick hits you on your head. First, you're lied to by a friend, then you finish work, and then a brick hits you on your head and kills you.

Elizabeth had to quit her job and get rid of Regreta. Elizabeth stared at the phone, indifferent emissary to the outside world. She was sleepy and hot. She got into the shower. The guy next door got into his shower. The water stopped running in her shower. He'd made a science of it, timed it. Maybe he wanted to be next to her. Pink tiles separated them. He was scrubbing, she was scrubbing. Maybe he'd heard her turn on the water, and the thought of it seeped through, he remembered he hadn't showered. The water pressure lowered. It got lower. The water trickled down. Oscar, she yelled, Oscar, wait a second. He turned off his water and waited. She rinsed. OK, she shouted. He started his water. It was a weird intimacy.

Oscar was a wiry Irish guy with a shaved head. He'd been in the States for years. He did odd jobs and had a string of girlfriends. They were all Irish. All the people who visited him or lived with him were Irish, Irish-American, or African-American. Oscar once played his music very loud, in the middle

of the night. They'd worked that out. It took a while, but they'd worked it out. He was all right. Except he showered when she did.

Roy and the dog went for a walk, coffee, the newspaper. Fatboy was a mutt. He wasn't fat, he was solid like Roy. When the two returned, Roy drank his coffee and fed Fatboy. Elizabeth was on the phone, talking to Larry.

—With families, you don't need enemies, she said.

Larry didn't have trouble sleeping.

Roy handed Elizabeth the *Times*. He took a shower—Oscar never showered at the same time as Roy—dressed for work, and walked to the door. They kissed. As soon as she touched his lips and smelled him, she wanted him to stay, But he left.

—It's not the heat, it's the humidity, Lizard, Roy said.

He locked the door behind him. Elizabeth went back to the table. Abandoned, Fatboy marched over to be petted.

New York, Friday, June 77, 1994. Late edition. Today, early clouds, then hazy, warm, humid. High 86. Tonight muggy, coastal fog. Low 75. Tomorrow, sultry. High 92. Yesterday, high 82, low 67. G.O.P. IN THE HOUSE IS TRYING TO BLOCK HEALTH CARE BILL. GENERALS OPPOSE COMBAT BY WOMEN. NEW YORK DEBATES ITSRULES FOR COMMITTING MENTALLY ILL. U.S. JURIES GROW TOUGHER ON THOSE SEEKING DAMAGES. QUEST FOR SAFER CIGARETTE NEVER REACHED GOAL. L.I.R.R. WORKERS GO ON STRIKE; COMMUTERS BRACE FOR GRIDLOCK. CLINTON MAY ADD G.I.'S IN KOREA WHILE REMAINING OPEN TO TALKS.

It wasn't a good death day. A newsworthy death was noted on page one, in a box, or the obituary itself started on page one. BRINGING BACK WOLVES was the box. There was a picture of a wolf, grinning. Thirty wolves were going to be reintroduced into Yellowstone National Park and Idaho. They could introduce them to Tompkins Square Park. Elizabeth smiled like a wolf at Fatboy. He stretched.

She turned to the obits first. Sports fans turn to the sports page for the scores. She was a death fan. She read every one, including the listings. She learned about the deaths of uncles and aunts of people she barely knew. Losses of high school friends she never saw. Some deaths consumed space. Famous figures. Infamous. Peculiar. Some deaths the living fought to have recognized by the *Times*. She knew of people who worried about how long their obits were going to be. They worried they wouldn't get a full column. They wanted a picture. Pictures were usually taken twenty years, on average, before the person's death, which meant the person's achievements were made twenty years before, then they disappeared from public view or they didn't want to be photographed later, older, otherwise there'd be a more recent picture available. Columns of print about the dead next to pictures of their relatively young faces.

His death may have been a suicide, technically, since he didn't choose extraordinary measures. He let himself die naturally. He didn't tell her of his wish for self death. Selfish death.

He said once, I'm not afraid to die. Death notices were straightforward. They paled next to the In Memoriams, addressed directly to the dead. Eerie, sad, silly, understandable, the way most things are.

"My heart is with you." The dead person was not going to read it, would never know this.

"I have never stopped thinking about you." Only the living would know that someone was thinking of her.

Elizabeth wondered what it meant to write direct addresses to the dead, for the living to read.

—I guess it's the thought that counts, she said to Roy yesterday.

—Yeah. But what's the thought?

In Memoriam. Told death to fuck itself, death fucks everybody but itself. Write if you can.

The coffee was bitter. She put another lemon peel in it and stirred again. Fatboy shook his tail. He wanted another walk. Elizabeth didn't want to take him. She didn't like scooping up his shit, especially in the summer.

A man comes home from the golf course. His wife says, Why do you look so depressed? The man says, Harry had a heart attack. His wife says, That's terrible. The man says, Yes, it was. All day long it was, hit the ball, drag Harry, hit the ball, drag Harry.

The void was outside her door. The stairs were an abyss of green sticky slime. There was an uncommonly strong, foul smell. It didn't seem to be the green slime. Someone may have died. The last time she thought someone or something was dead in the building, because of a smell wafting up from below her wooden floor, she figured a dead rat or pigeon was decomposing, and she went downstairs and asked her neighbors if they smelled something dead. They said they were cooking. They were a little distant after that. Roy said, What'd you expect.

Elizabeth was stymied in front of her door. She locked it. Ernest trotted jauntily down the stairs. They met at her landing. It was the first time in months.

—What's that stench? Elizabeth asked.

—There's a guy sleeping at my door. I'm still running a homeless shelter, Ernest said.

—Even in the summer?

—No accounting.

They walked down the filthy stairs together. Cigarettes, a used condom, gum wrappers, dried gum blackened with time. It didn't stick anymore. Nothing big. The smell became worse.

Ernest clutched *The Confessions of St. Augustine* to his chest.

—If there's a heat wave, he said. All the garbage . . .

—Don't say it. *The Confessions*?

—I once wanted to be a priest.

—Do you still go to confession?

—Sure. Catholics go to confession.

—That's good.

There was blood on the vestibule floor. Crack vials. The smell was overwhelming. There was a pile of shit near a bunch of takeout menus pushed behind the door.

The smell was coming from upstairs and downstairs.

Elizabeth was nauseated, speechless. Ernest understood. They looked into each other's eyes and stepped over the shit. Probably human shit. Some of the crackheads came back and shit on your floor if you pushed them out of the vestibule, or were too tough with them. It was retribution. It could've been the peroxided one. She was out to get Elizabeth.

—Nice, Ernest said.

—Lovely, Elizabeth said.

She held her nose. Ernest said he'd call the landlord about getting a new door. If there was a good lock on the outside door, the dopesters and crackheads wouldn't get in, and the homeless man wouldn't be able to get up the stairs and sleep on the top landing.

Elizabeth and Ernest were on the street, in front of the lousy door.

—I've tried, Elizabeth said.

—I'll give it another whirl, he said.

—Good luck, she said.

—Good luck, he said.

Ernest smiled grimly.

Hector was outside, too, on the sidewalk, conspiring with the Big G.

—Not our day, Elizabeth whispered.

—I'm not ready for this, Ernest said.

Ernest walked one way, she walked the other. She had to pass the Big G and Hector. This is my street, they're not going to make me run, Elizabeth encouraged herself. She marched past them, eyes straight ahead. She controlled her breathing. In, out, in, out, in, out. Calm, even breaths. She kept herself from jumping up and down on the sidewalk and screaming, There's shit in the vestibule, Hector. Human shit.

It was late morning. Elizabeth felt late and good-for-nothing. Her mother said she was a good-for-nothing. She agreed with her mother about some things.

Elizabeth walked on, into the day. The endless night had oozed, drooled into day. There may have been people who despised her on sight, or who had grown to dislike her over the years, or who never even noticed her though they passed her on the street every day. But she was ignorant of them. She headed east toward Avenue A, toward the park.

Tyrone was coming toward her.

—Hey, Elizabeth, let me wash your windows. I'll do them today.

Tyrone always had a wave and a big smile for Elizabeth. Hector and the Big G were watching, she knew they were. So was Frankie.

Everyone knew Tyrone. He was a big, friendly black guy, almost a giant. Tyrone was retarded. He hung around the neighborhood, their building especially. He appeared out of nowhere. He needed work. He wanted to clean the halls of their building.

Tyrone told Elizabeth he lived in Brooklyn. Sometimes he couldn't get home because he didn't have a token. She lent him money and told him she didn't want it back. He always tried to pay her back. He'd grab her hand, shake it and hold it. He needed affection, to be touched. She'd shake his hand and then, after he'd passed by, she'd wave her hand in the air. She didn't think she'd catch something. He was a sad case.

—I'll wash your windows, I'll do your windows, today, anytime, Tyrone said.

—No no. No, thanks, she said.

—I'll do a good job, you'll see.

—I'll pay you if you do it.

—You'll see how clean I can get them.

—No no, Tyrone. Thanks, but no, not today.

—You don't have to pay me. I'll do a good job.

Voluntary servitude alarmed her, she'd been a volunteer. She'd had other slavish offers, to rub her back, massage her feet, do her floors, suck her cunt, whatever. She didn't take them up, not for long, anyway. It's easy to be a casual sadist.

She didn't want the pleasure. A man's face, blurry, ashen, a trashy hotel room, a bottle of Jack Daniel's, picture imperfect, sounds muted, the tape played often, had worn itself out, rubbed itself out. It speeded up and slowed down, and the pictures were smeared, run through too often, everything in pieces, he doesn't matter. Rocket to oblivion. She didn't want that. No sense to it, she thought. He tried to take me down with him, but in the end I ruined him. He's a ruined man today, Elizabeth remembered contentedly.

Everyone should confess.

Sometimes Hector used Tyrone to clean the halls. He probably didn't pay him, or he paid him next to nothing. Hector permitted

Tyrone to do it, gave him the chance to work, because he didn't want to bother to do it himself. Tyrone needed approval, so he'd do anything. You have to be in pretty bad shape yourself, reduced to petty inhumanities, to take advantage of retarded people. Hector was oppressed and oppressive.

Tyrone would clean the halls and stairs. But since he hadn't been properly hired—the Big G didn't know or wouldn't approve, Hector should be doing it, it was his job—Tyrone's work had to be accomplished surreptitiously. Tyrone didn't have access to a sink and clean water. He'd mop the six floors with the same bucket of dirty water. The dirt was pushed around, spread from corner to corner. Elizabeth always thanked him, because the floors looked a little better, the dirt was diluted, thinned into dark streaks. All Tyrone wanted was to be thanked.

When Elizabeth offered Tyrone money for cleaning the halls, he refused. He seemed hurt by her offer. Offended. He'd say no, and awkwardly offer his big hand to shake hers, and they'd shake, and then she'd walk away. She tried not to look back, then she did. He'd be smiling at her and nodding his head.

Today, he held her there. She was trapped. Tyrone showed her pictures of his wedding. Maybe his wife was slightly retarded too. They both looked blissfully or uncomfortably out of it. Tyrone was happy about the wedding. Marriage was the highpoint of many people's lives. It was pathetic. She thought she should buy Tyrone a present. Roy would tell her not to get any more involved than she was. Elizabeth had as many compunctions as compulsions.

What do you call a midget psychic on the lam?

What?

Small medium at large.

Tyrone reminded her of the money slave. Roy and his friend Joe hooked up with the money slave years ago. Joe saw an ad in the Village Voice about earning money writing music reviews, no experience necessary. Joe and Roy contacted him. Easy money.

It was a hustle. The money slave wanted another kind of transaction—he wanted them to make him work, wanted them to order him to work, he demanded them to force him over the telephone to work harder for them, to make him make money for them, to take two jobs, even three, to support them. He paid them to say that. He phoned them, and they'd accommodate him.

They met with him in person occasionally. The money slave would hand over the money he'd asked Roy and Joe to order him to earn for them. Elizabeth followed Roy to one of his meets with the money slave, at the World Trade Center. From behind a column she watched Roy make the exchange with the money slave. He was an average-looking white guy, a low-level Wall Street suit.

Roy was supposed to be the money slave's master. It's hard to be a master if you're not trained for it. There's an art to everything. The money slave probably didn't have a family to make demands on him or to give purpose and meaning to a life of pallid corporate indenture. He was a lonely guy with strange, memorable desires. He explained to Roy, If you made me take a second job, that would make you the most important thing in my life.

One day when the money slave was groveling, squealing, on the phone—Tell me to work harder, tell me, tell me to take a third job to support you, tell me, make me work harder for you—suddenly Roy couldn't control himself. He laughed. The money slave was insulted, embarrassed. He hung up. He never called again. Roy lost the gig. The money slave paid for his own brand of humiliation. He had needs, desires. The city offered him anonymity. He could buy workers, substitutes. When he wanted, who, where, what kind, for how long. Roy laughed at an inappropriate moment. He couldn't keep it up, even for the money.

That was a while ago.

Someone else's fantasy is a joke, a comedy.

Tyrone walked west. The Big G and Hector trapped him. They were talking to him. The Big G was shaking a hypocritical white finger at him. They'd castigate him, Gloria especially, she'd mete out some punishment for him, and call it work. The Big G didn't want him around, Hector did if he could use him. Tyrone was unpredictable, but he was harmless.

Yelping boys from the Boys Club were being rounded up and put on buses to summer camp to keep them from becoming murderers. A two-week idyll in the country for the underprivileged. The underprivileged's mothers, fathers, aunts, uncles, sisters, brothers were hanging around, sad, bored, impatient, happy, waiting to wave good-bye. The Boys Club was tied to the police. They could do anything.

Tompkins Square Park was leafy and green. The trees' shadows marked sidewalk oases. Mothers, fathers, and assorted child-care workers parked themselves on benches near the sandpit. They had their stations and watched their kids. They fanned themselves.

After the cops' attack on the park squatters one summer night, which was like living in Salvador for that night, with a helicopter whirring overhead and tear gas and hundreds of people running and hundreds of police chasing them, and after the cleanup of the park, which was closed for a year, its entrances transformed into Checkpoint Charlies, the sandbox was free of dog and human shit. No one argued about that.

A few park insurgents were asleep under lightweight blankets. It was quiet.

Ernest had wanted to be a priest. It killed her. Ernest needed to right their situation. He was a spiritual guy. He believed in God, Christ, and the Virgin. God was closing the century. The Crusades would look like the Easter parade.

The Hispanic guy from the bike store was repairing bikes on the sidewalk.

Ernest was propelled by faith and God's grace. He was deluded, millions of people were. Huge numbers of people. Religion made her sick. Supreme beings and redemption. People expected to be redeemed like bottles or recycled, to return as birds or dogs or grains of sand, and go on and on. Ernest needed to make things right. She really didn't care why.

The smell of beer, pungent and musty, oozed to the pavement from the bars. At Brownies tonight: 700 Miles and Hooch. Elizabeth liked being in bars just before they were full. Nothing like a bar. Nothing like a bartender. Nothing like loose talk. People she knew weren't drinking much. Everyone wanted to be in control. The older you got, that's all you had, control.

Being out of control was better, blasted and wasted, telling tales on telltale nights, on the brink of sex with a stranger with intense eyes and a mad laugh. On the brink of losing everything. Heartless, homeless. Some were never there, couldn't touch the edge, live at the bottom, do some bottom feeding. Nothing adventured, everything lost. Nothing ventured without losing something else. Avoiding failure, even a whiff of failure, they didn't think about the past. They say they don't miss anything, didn't miss anything, have no regrets. They did what they wanted. Elizabeth giggled, then she held herself in check, held back.

People don't expose their need the way Ernest does. It was confused with being needy. That's why there was so much impotence, girlfriends complaining about flaccidity. Years ago a man told her, after she'd rejected him, that as he grew older, he was learning to enjoy the luxury of impotence. Impotence and failure are luxuries. Most people can't afford them.

It was muggy. She didn't expect to be mugged in weather like this. Too liquid and slow for jumping on someone, except the most desperate, too enervating. Her skin was coated with light sweat. Elizabeth didn't like to sweat unless she was having sex.

How do you know when the stage is level?
When drool is coming out of both sides of the drummer's mouth.

Five Catholic schoolboys were tossing a basketball in the school's parking lot. They were lousy, black, yellow, white, lumbering to the basket, clumsy. A few nuns were watching their charges. Their white hands were crossed over their short habits and rested on full stomachs. The school's mural: "Mary Help of Christian School, Give

Me Souls Take Away The Rest." It was painted blue, covered a wall. A cartoon portrait of Mary and Jesus surrounded by saints and souls. Have mercy. Take away the rest. It was a time without mercy. People who believe in the soul don't think anyone else has one. Maybe Ernest did. Fear the righteous. They have no pity.

The Metropolitan Funeral Parlor had most of the body-and-soul business in the neighborhood. It wasn't where Emilia's wake was held. There were no coffins on the sidewalk this morning, no crowd, no crying, no limos. Elizabeth hated passing by the mean and morose scene when the hearse was waiting for its next coffin, and family and friends were crying, clustered in small groups to console each other, and the hearse drivers were lounging around with cigarettes dangling from their mouths, bored out of their skulls. People were grieving in another world, not theirs.

He didn't have a funeral. He was cremated in another city. They held a memorial service for him later. It was hard to cry after a while. Elizabeth was toughening up, she was hardening with age, becoming brittle, like her nails. They broke more easily. Didn't everything. Can't take everything on. Have to take some of it on. The morons. The shit in the vestibule.

The sad-eyed gray-haired man was settled in his chair at the window of the printing shop. He chewed on a cigar. PREMISES CONTROLLED BY ATTACK DOGS. She'd never seen any. He was a daily enigma. Maybe a concentration camp survivor. She might work for the tragic old man one day. She'd spend hours proofreading, because no one in the shop was good at it, she'd choose typefaces for wedding, birth, and death announcements and listen to the relentless purr, chug, and whir of the printing press. The smell of ink and cigars would linger in the air, they'd all argue about politics, discuss the local news, how terrible the mayor was, how bad it was when the squatters were assaulted, how everyone deserved it or didn't, whatever they got, in one way or another. Then they'd close up shop at the end of the day. Everyone would gather round.

—Remember Howard Beach?

—Always sounded like a person to me before. . .

—It's not like Germany, the old man'd say.

—They chased him across the highway. . .

—Can't even live your life, the black printer would say.

—Racist cowards, she'd say.

—Howard Beach. . .

The printer's dark arms would be smeared with purple ink.

—And Crown Heights?

—A kid run over. . .

—It was an accident. . .

—A car runs a light. . .

—Mayor Dinkins shoulda . . .

—The ambulance ignored . . .

—Dinkins did the right thing . . .

—But the trial was a mockery, the old man would say.

His voice would wane. He'd wander back to his chair, slump into it. His melancholy was physical. Elizabeth would return to proofreading, the black printer would go back to setting type. The receptionist and designer would settle in too. The next day it would all begin again. She'd become fixed and old in one place, one job.

The public school kids should've been in school. The usual characters were hanging out on the corners. The runners weren't out.

126

Only the hard-core desperadoes with eyes like pins. They disappeared into chaotic rooms and emerged and disappeared again. Their eyes darted everywhere. Crackheads strode ramrod stiff, up and down the block, arms up, out, and down, like Nazi salutes, involuntary movements. They were on patrol. The nod squad arrived later. The crackheads were fueled with synthetic energy. They had nowhere to go, hunters and gatherers prowling in circles.

One lesbian frog says to another, You're right, we do taste like chicken.

Gisela limped onto A from Twelfth Street. Her dog limped along beside her.
—It is a terrible time, now. Look what happens again!
Gisela's face was dotted with scars, old wounds. There were a few fresh wounds. She had picked them. Elizabeth stared at the red holes, windows to the soul. Gisela's skin was clearer than it was the last time she'd seen her.
—A woman is trying to destroy me. See, my dog is sick. She is poisoning my dog. I went away and she was supposed to take care of him and look at him. Look at his rash.
Gisela pointed to a scabby, hairless patch on the dog's rump. It made Elizabeth sick.
—Why's the woman poisoning your dog? Elizabeth asked.
—It's the Swiss government.
—They're after you again?
—Ach. My mother's legacy. They thought I knew too much because a lot of very heavy people in the government were

involved with my mother. My mother was exploited by them.

—You mean, the heroin dealing she was forced to do?

—They are very liberal with drugs because the government is involved, and that means money for them. My mother was working under a lawyer, in Zurich, who was a good friend with a man from the parliament, who was negotiating with the Syrian extremist groups in Argentina. They have a big colony of Syrian extremists. They were afraid that I knew about it. I didn't know about it. They were afraid I would talk too much. I didn't know anything. At that time.

Gisela shifted from one leg to the other. Elizabeth had heard some of the story. Gisela shifted again.

—Your leg hurts?

—They want to operate, and I always say. . .

—What kind of operation?

—To replace my hip. I always say no, I need first intensive therapy. I'm very weak, I'm falling apart. In Cuba, for the first time I met a doctor who agreed with me. When I say this to a doctor, he doesn't want to hear of it.

A bicycle messenger zipped past them on the sidewalk.

—I couldn't sleep last night, Elizabeth said.

—It's the neighborhood, Gisela said.

—It's pushing me over the edge.

—Compared to what I went through, it's paradise. It's beautiful, Switzerland, but I went through shit there. Those people are not human beings. They're worse than Nazis. Here, you see, I'm happy. I keep my distance because I cannot tell my story. I get along. They leave me alone. They respect me. I respect them. I have no problem. I have my peace of mind.

—That's important.

—I was fine here, until 1973, that's when I collapsed. I was accused of being involved in drugs, which wasn't true. Then I had a terrible, terrible love affair. Men never meant much in my life, believe me. I did not even love him. It was like he was doing black magic to me. It was the first time in my life, I was thirty-six. It was horrible. I just collapsed.

—Then your hip went out?

—From standing on my feet too long. But I had a problem before. I was beaten up by the police in 1964 when I was arrested.

—In Switzerland?

—I didn't pay my hospital bill in India. I had enough money to pay for an Indian hospital, but they said that I was white and I had to go to a luxury hospital. I knew in advance I couldn't pay. Then one night the troops came and picked me up and kidnapped me and took me to Switzerland where I got beaten up very badly. They went inside me to see if I had drugs, of course I had no drugs. I was in the hospital. And they beat me up, to make sure I would spit out drugs. But I had my hip problem even before.

—How did it start?

—Child abuse. I went through hell, but I'm happy to be here.

Elizabeth knew she should get going.

—My family didn't want to have anything to do with me. First of all because I was my mother's daughter, and because I look like her. I look exactly like her. Except I'm lighter, My mother was of gypsy background. So was my father.

—They're gypsies?

—French Huguenot, but of gypsy background. I am so light, my
family didn't want to have anything to do with me. They're
assimilated.

—When did they give up their gypsy ways?

—When they became Huguenots in the fifteenth century. They
were kicked out of Spain and became French Huguenots.
People don't know that the Huguenot religion was founded by
the Jews and the gypsies and the Arabs, who were kicked out
of Spain. The Catholic religion didn't believe in money, but the
Protestants believe in money. The Thirty Years War was based
on this, it was a money issue. The so-called religious war.

Elizabeth was tempted to melt with Gisela on the sidewalk. She
could lose herself in salty, humid dispiritedness.

—What happened to your mother?

—I have no idea. Yesterday I told my social worker that my first
memory was of my mother, how beautiful she was.

Elizabeth scrutinized Gisela's dry, pale skin.

—Are you eating OK?

—To tell you the truth, I'm so depressed since my burglary, I
don't eat right. I eat bagels, with cheese, butter. I do eat a lot of
fruits. I drink water a lot.

—Your skin is looking a little better.

—Because I'm over that problem. My soul is better.

—About losing your children years ago?

—All of that. That's why my skin looks better.

—I don't want children.

—I didn't want them, they just didn't have abortions, and no protection in those days. I was a runaway, and somebody took advantage. It wasn't rape. I was raped later on.

Gisela looked down the street. There was some commotion on the corner. They watched it together. A couple of boys were being territorial. No weapons. It broke up.

—Thank God, I'm rent-controlled. If I lose my apartment, that's it. I don't go out, I stay home. I only walk the dog. You don't see me.

—Not much.

—Because I only go to the doctor or grocery shopping, I walk the dog, that's about it.

—It's good to get exercise.

Elizabeth hardly ever exercised. She walked. Gisela thought about something else, Elizabeth could see some caution, storm alert arrows, crossing her face, and then the concern passed, or Gisela pushed it away.

—Don't you ever complain about a social worker. They have more power than you think.

Elizabeth didn't have a social worker. She complained to the wrong people on the block. Elizabeth didn't tell Gisela about her problems with the young super, Gloria, or Hector. Gisela shifted her weight from one leg to the other. Her dog was hunkered down on the hot sidewalk. He looked miserable. It was jungle humid. Gisela glanced at her dog, then at Elizabeth. She ignored her pain.

—In Switzerland, everybody who's a humanist ends up in a mental hospital, because they don't want human beings. There are only banks and insurance. The guy who was the founder of the Red Cross, Jean-Henri Dunant, he ended up in a mental hospital too. I go now.

Gisela brought things to a conclusion with flair. She started to move. She glanced at Elizabeth again.

—You look good today. Yah.

Gisela appreciated Elizabeth's appearance. It didn't matter if Elizabeth hadn't slept through a scarred night that might've terminated in her loss of control, a night that could've resulted in her assassinating someone. Gisela's version of reality was unique, cut to fit. Everyone's was. Most versions were less radically altered than Gisela's. Gisela wasn't about fashion. She had style. You had it or you didn't.

Elizabeth didn't argue with anyone's style or experience. Only sometimes with what it meant. Gisela, as she herself put it, was rent-controlled. Elizabeth was rent-stabilized. Elizabeth would look up Jean-Henri Dunant in the proofroom. The room had a reference library. They had to check themselves before they corrected anyone else, to find the rectitude or error of their own ways first.

What's the difference between Chinese food and Jewish restaurants?

With Chinese food, after an hour, you're hungry again. In a Jewish restaurant, after an hour, you're still eating.

She had to lose the friend and the job.

In Memoriam. If you hanged yourself, I'd feel guilty for a minute. Then I'd get over it. All the smiles in your repertoire can't sugarcoat your treachery. You deserve yourself.

Elizabeth approached the scraggly little tree in front of a popular bodega. Most people on the west side of Avenue A congregated there. She nodded to some of the men. Sometimes Hector played cards with a couple of them. They sat out in front at a table. Hector always lifted his hat and tipped it when he saw her. He was courteous. His hat-tipping inspired panic in Elizabeth.

The scraggly little tree was enclosed by wire mesh. It was home to penned-in chickens and a duck. They had a plastic tub of water they could jump into. They couldn't wade. They couldn't fly or run. They had each other. They looked sick.

—Sweet chickens, cute duck, Elizabeth said to a man.

He was dropping lettuce leaves into the enclosure.

—Si.

—They're yours?

—Si, they're mine.

—They're sweet.

—The children like them.

Hope you're not going to eat them, she nearly said. They were too sick to eat, even if he wanted to.

Three ruined alcoholics graced the corner. They were slumped in their usual places. Three men sprawled or asleep on the ground. Occasionally a woman. Swollen, red, black-and-blue faces are more awful in the heat. One man was holding the morning's pint. He passed it around. They stayed close to the liquor store, but not too close. They lay next door to the corner slice-of-pizza store. It had a cat in its doorway. Elizabeth never talked to any of them. They vomited all over the corner.

He didn't throw up, he held his liquor, walked in his sleep in tacky hotel rooms that I thought were cool. I could've become pregnant. He wanted a kid, he'd left one already. I would've had an abortion. He was drunk all the time. They didn't have abortions for Gisela. All her kids gone, dead, if she really had them.

Four chaplains in an authoritarian army are playing poker. It's forbidden. A colonel walks into the room and they quickly put away the cards. The colonel takes a Bible and asks each one to swear he wasn't playing poker. The priest puts his hand on the Bible and swears he wasn't. The Buddhist monk puts his hand on the Bible and shakes his head no. The minister swears he wasn't. The rabbi places his hand on the Bible and asks, Have you ever seen a person play poker alone?

Earl wasn't at the door in front of the post office. Geraldo, the guy with the patch over one eye, was guarding their position. It was a heavily contested beggars' site. It'd belonged to Earl and Geraldo, the Hispanic pirate, for a while now. Elizabeth had been leery of Geraldo and partial to Earl. Now she favored both with small donations.

Earl was an elderly black man. He'd lost his job years back and could never find another one. He'd lost his wife, his children. He'd been robbed of everything. Sometimes in the summers he worked in hotels as a dishwasher. That's probably where he was now, unless he was in the hospital. He was sick a lot. His brown skin turned gray in the winter.

—Don't have change now. Later maybe, she said.

—OK, Liz.

—Where's Earl?

—Don't know.

—He hasn't been around. Is he in the hospital?

—Don't know. I'll see what I can find out.

The line was long. It was always long. But the post office was air-conditioned. The woman who heard voices coming from her post office box wasn't there. She was plagued, a movie star down on her luck. She rubbed orange rouge all over her white cheeks and wore lace gloves. Always a sign of derangement. The woman complained loudly and bitterly about the roles that were taken away from her, she protested vehemently, glaring into her postbox, against the post office. It was holding back her mail, it was losing her mail. It was the government's fault her movie career had stalled. It was a government plot. Everyone on line sort of sympathized with her attack on the efficiency of the post office. You didn't have to be schizophrenic to nod in absentminded agreement.

The mental movie star wasn't around.

Elizabeth stood on a line. There was no movement.

—Put more people on. I have to go to work, a woman yelled.

—Yeah, yeah, let's get moving, a man seconded.

—This is terrible, Elizabeth said.

—Patience is a virtue, a woman said to Elizabeth.

—I have no virtues, Elizabeth said.

Nothing happened. The line grew. Air conditioning didn't help. Everyone became hot under the collar. Elizabeth used to go to the manager's window and ask to speak to the supervisor, but it took time to roust the supervisor. She hated wasting her life on line. Everyone did.

There were three windows open out of six. There was a new worker at one window, a young, eager, and good-looking black woman. Elizabeth sympathized with workers on their first day on the job.

Elizabeth wanted to mail a small package and buy a book of stamps. The new worker weighed the package. She pulled open a drawer and grabbed a book of stamps. She struggled to lift up a few loose stamps for the package. Then she dropped all the stamps on the counter and took the package off the scale.

The new worker couldn't grasp the stamps, she couldn't pick them up off the counter. Her extremely long nails curled under and hit the surface of the counter. she couldn't put her fingertips on the stamps. The nails repelled her from doing that. She tried using one nail, like a shovel, and then she used two nails, like tweezers. Finally she resorted to sliding the stamps off the counter with her palm—fingers out, nails curling to infinity—into her other palm. Somehow she pasted the stamps on the package. The young woman beamed triumphantly at Elizabeth.

The line now snaked three times around the post office. It was the new worker. She was supposed to speed service. She was hindering it. Teeth clenched, Elizabeth walked to the supervisor's window. She rang a bell and waited. An overweight white man in a cheap suit came toward the window. He walked very slowly. He had mustard stains on his maroon tie.

—Yes? the manager said, already annoyed.

—There's a new woman working a window.

—Yes?

—She's OK, but I don't know what the civil service laws are

about discriminating. . .

—Discriminating?

—About personal stuff . . .

—Personal?

—The woman has very long nails. I don't know if this is discriminating, long nails. It's not discrimination. . . it's about regulations. . . The point is, she can't pick up the stamps.

The manager was bored. He listened without comprehension.

—See the line? Elizabeth asked, exasperated.

—I see it.

—It's very long.

—So?

—The new woman can't pick up the stamps. She physically can't pick them up and put them on the mail and something should be done. I don't know what the regulations are about personal dress. . .

—Dress?

—Nail length.

There was a long pause. They were at an impasse.

—I'll check into it, he said, finally.

—She could do a good job, she just needs to be told that long nails aren't. . .

The manager wanted her to go away, to evaporate, to shut up. Nail length probably wasn't itemized under the dress code. It wasn't simple like smoking in the workplace.

People with long nails have them to show they don't do manual labor. They might also imagine that dead cells jutting out of their fingers is attractive. The young woman hadn't realized the post office required light manual labor. Elizabeth didn't know if the young woman could do a good job. She gave her the benefit of the doubt. She didn't want her fired for the length of her nails.

Lesbians cut their nails short. Hands and nails were a dyke thing. Let them take over the post office, Elizabeth thought. She'd phone Chris. Chris wouldn't want to work in the post office. No one did. It was disabling because everyone thought you were disabled.

Elizabeth grabbed her mail from the postbox and raced out. She hoped the new worker hadn't seen her talking to the supervisor.

A man smelling of cheap perfume rushed in. His face was pink. He brushed her body with his body. He'd been freshly shaved at the barber. He was round and pink. He brushed against her twice.

—Sorry, he said.

—That's OK.

—Sorry, he said again.

He looked familiar.

—Who's that? Elizabeth asked Geraldo the pirate.

—Don't know. I've seen him before though.

Elizabeth dropped two quarters into Geraldo's worn paper cup. She'd heard about an Anglo-Pakistani writer visiting New York. He noticed a black man holding a cup on a platform in the subway. The writer dropped a quarter into his cup. The man said, That's my coffee, idiot.

Subways were fast. She could read on the subway. Elizabeth rode the subway during the day. Not at night. Large men spread their legs across two seats. Small men also took up two subway seats. They did it differently from big men. Small men hunched and pushed their bodies forward, shoving as much of their bulk forward as they could, they even bulked up, made as much of themselves as they could. Some big teenaged girls took up two seats on purpose and very fat people took up two, sometimes three seats, not on purpose. But subway riders hated them anyway. She did.

Sitting next to one of the big or small men, squeezed between two strangers, Elizabeth forced her fury down. She could choke on it. She could become violent. She squeezed into whatever space was available. She made them as uncomfortable as she could. She was uncomfortable too. She was crushed between strangers. It was a violation of the unknown kind. Her knees were locked together. She was perched on the seat, the way she sat on the toilet. She couldn't breathe. She might explode. She could just as easily have thrust a knife into the guy's chest and cut out his heart as asked the civil question, Will you please close your legs?

She did once, but like going out onto the street and telling the young super to stop revving his engine at six A.M., she would never again ask a man on the subway to close his legs.

When the question escaped from her mouth, it popped, and sex sprayed out. Sex was lying there in the question like his enormous legs across two seats. She'd ejaculated and startled them both, startled the whole car. The big guy shut his legs fast. Then the two of them continued to sit next to each other, primly, as if they'd just had bad sex. Elizabeth suffered for the whole ride. It was a worthless victory.

She wouldn't do that again. She didn't enjoy the ride better anyway, crushed and infuriated. She stood. She would stand. She couldn't read standing. She'd occasionally glare at the offenders. She didn't try to sit down next to them. She hung on to a metal strap. The legspreaders put their newspapers up in front of their faces. They turned the volume up on their cassette players. They zoned her out. She didn't exist to them.

Two bags of vomit are walking around the neighborhood. One bag of vomit starts to cry. The other bag of vomit asks, What's the matter? The first bag of vomit says, I was brought up around here.

Elizabeth drifted in front of the newsstand. She had her hand out. It had a dollar in it. The beautiful Indian woman wasn't there. There were only two Indian men. People were buying lottery tickets in back. One of the men took the dollar.

—Where's the woman? Elizabeth asked.

—Ah, she's away, one answered.

—Away?

—Yes, she's home.

—Is she coming back?

—She will stay home.

—Tell her hello for me, please.

—I will tell her.

Elizabeth received fifty cents change for the *New York Post*; "O.J.'S TEARS: ANGIUSHED STAR ATTENDS EX-WIFE'S FUNERAL AS COPS TIGHTEN THE NET." The Indian woman had seemed content selling newspapers. When the man said good-bye to her, Elizabeth viewed him with suspicion. It was an unguarded moment. "KNICKS SET FOR CRUCIAL GAME 5 TONIGHT."

Kenny was waving to her. Her former mail carrier was a short black man from the Bronx. The post office gave Kenny another route after he'd had her route for ten years. He was taken off it, just like that. Kenny had grown attached to the block, knew their names, their mail. He couldn't sleep for a while, he was so distressed.

—No one thinks mail carriers have feelings about our routes.

We do. Ten years. I know you ten years. Almost eleven.

His new route was still in the neighborhood.

—Hey, Kenny.

—How you keeping?

—So so. You?

—My mother's ailing.

—Sorry.

—Praying she'll be all right.

Kenny lifted a hefty pack of mail from his blue cart and unlocked the door to a five-story building. He disappeared. In his cart lay thousands of envelopes. Some would change the fortunes of their recipients. Mail carriers were important. They brought messages to the block.

Maybe the Indian woman had a fatal disease. The man wouldn't tell Elizabeth.

The public telephones were being guarded by some of the goons. You couldn't make a call. They'd say, We're waiting and stand there impassively, aggressively. They didn't have remotes. You were supposed to wait patiently until they received their call and their orders to move. There was nothing else to do. You didn't want to get capped just because you wanted to use a pay phone.

How do you know when your dad is fucking your sister in the ass? His dick tastes of shit.

Elizabeth almost fell on the music junkie. He had a fish-shaped guitar. He was hitting on two teenaged girls. One of the girls sneezed. They were trying to get away from him.

—You're allergic to me, and I was just going to ask you to marry me, he said.

The girls giggled. A scab-faced junkie could mention marriage and raise giggles and blushes. Elizabeth didn't give him money. Except the other day when she saw him, bloodied, forehead bandaged like the head of a revolutionary soldier, and his fish-shaped guitar wasn't hanging down his skinny back, so then she gave him money. The cops had taken his guitar. He was dead to everything but dope and his tinny, fish guitar. He'd be dead soon enough, he wouldn't bother anyone.

I wouldn't want to talk to him for a minute, and I'm giving him money. He'd just whine, like the almost-dead woman who walks around here, scuffling, bent over, bent in half, begging in a subhuman voice, no one wants to give her anything, no one wants to listen, no one can stand her, no one wants to keep her alive, she's like an infection. It's a disease, narcissism of the afflicted. She'd talk your ear off if you let her.

The Mexican take-out and sit-down was a cold hole in the wall. Elizabeth ordered a cheese enchilada. She thought it'd go down. She sat down. A rookie cop walked in. He ordered too and sat down next to her. His gun stuck out from his waist. He was wearing his vest. He was corseted and rosy-cheeked. The vest was the new model.

He was freshly shaved. He was overheating, stuffed and split like a boiled hot dog.

Elizabeth was ready to confess. She asked him if he'd seen any crossbows and arrows lately. The cop looked at her, the way cops do at civilians who aren't perceived as immediate threats, the way experts look at amateurs, and the cop responded, not to her question, which was too silly for him even to consider. She saw his frustration. It colored his pink cheeks pinker.

—I'm useless, they can round up all the legal handguns, because most murders aren't committed with legal firearms, the murderers don't use legal guns.

He thought hard.

—And another thing, don't get me started . . .

She didn't say a word.

—The thieves are laughing at me. I try to arrest someone for breaking into a car, and they say, Why you picking on me? Go after the murderers. I'm not murdering anybody. There are bad guys out there. I'm not doing anything, I'm not hurting anyone. You know. No one's got morals anymore.

The cop rested his elbows on the table. He opened his hands wide. She could see his palms. She looked for his fate line. It wasn't there. He breathed hard. His vest didn't move. His order—rice, beans, and a beef taco—was ready.

—Here's a different case. What about that junkie with the fish-shaped guitar? The cops took his guitar from him.

—Don't know about that, I didn't hear about that, the cop said.

He was chewing.

—He begs. You guys took away his fish guitar.

143

—I didn't.

—I'm not accusing you personally, but what's the principle. You take away his livelihood. . .

—What's a fisherman. . .

—He's a junkie with a fish-shaped. . .

—You don't know what the guy was doing. You think you see things. Civilians don't. You don't. Believe me. Us cops. . .I seen things that'd make your stomach turn. Believe me.

He looked down at his rice and beans. He stared at his plate listlessly.

—I believe you, Elizabeth said.

The deaf tenant, Herbert, walked in. Elizabeth wanted the cop to keep talking. She wanted to gain his trust, reach out to him, and have him unfold like a clean sheet, or a dirty one, and she'd see the marks, he'd reveal secrets he'd never told anyone. She lusted for his illicit cop secrets.

She didn't know how far she could go with the cop, and now that Herbert from the twin building had arrived, though he was very deaf—they mouthed hello—Elizabeth felt uneasier talking to a cop. She was white, the cop was white, Herbert was black, and what would Herbert think, not that he'd hear, for all he knew she could be cursing the rookie, calling the pink-faced cop a pig. The cop was porky.

Herbert's face betrayed no trace of anything. It was placid. He was a calm guy, and he calmly ordered and sat down near the cop. His deafness kept him separate, maybe. Herbert said hello to the cop. It was cozy. A small place. Maybe they knew each other.

—Herbert, we've got to talk about the situation, Elizabeth said.

She mouthed and mimed the words and put her hand to her ear.

—OK, he shouted.

—We have no services anymore.

—Me too.

The cop didn't pay attention. He stuffed his face. The food was salty. Mexicans know how to live in a hot climate. The cop was driven to be what he was, a master, a slave. He wanted to police the city, to do good. Ever since he was a kid, he wanted to be a cop, his father was a cop, his brothers, and he saw his job as trying to stop someone from making other people miserable when they find their car stolen or smashed and have to spend days with the insurance company, and their insurance goes up. Through no fault of their own. Most people didn't have theft insurance on old cars. The porky cop wanted to make the world better. He was misguided. Who wasn't.

Herbert might not agree with this.

Elizabeth ate her cheese enchilada quickly. She always ate fast. She wished she'd taken the cop's badge number or last name. She could call him at the station in the middle of the night.

—Officer, I'm the woman who talked to you in the Mexican restaurant the other day. You had a beef taco. I had a cheese enchilada. Remember? Anyway, I'm about to murder someone who's making noise, and throwing garbage everywhere, the guy's a menace, and he's been driving me crazy, because I can't sleep, and I can't be responsible. Arrest me because I'm going to kill him. Through no fault of my own. I waive my rights. I can't be human. Maybe that's what I am, too human, you know?

She probably wouldn't get philosophical with him.

There was nothing big between her and the cop, nothing much between her impulse to reach for his gun and his impulse to stop her, shoot her in the head or hand, between her need for authority and his need to be an authority, her need for help and his need to help, her desire for protection and his desire for heroic action, and vice versa. It could be breached by a whisper, Let me touch your gun. There were fine lines not only crisscrossing her face, double crossing her, and what, if anything, would make her cross the fine, pine line. What if anything—the lawyer's anything—what if anything did you have on your mind the night you shot an arrow into young blah's head?

I'm God's mail carrier, I had a letter to deliver from him. She was losing it, whatever it was. She wasn't really looking, she really wasn't looking for herself. She hoped no one was looking for her. Especially the law.

She'd been close to criminals, she'd lived with one, Mitch, he was probably mildly retarded. He wore cowboy boots. He was from Oklahoma and came by his outfits the hard way. One day he disappeared and wrote her a note—she was in college—he could barely write. He was probably on Death Row now. She wasn't, although everyone had to walk the walk eventually. She'd never been addicted or habituated except to Valium and amphetamine, on prescription. It was unlikely she'd go to jail.

She said good-bye to the cop and Herbert. The cop glanced up. He didn't seem to know she was there anymore. He shouldn't be on the street. The clock was ticking for this guy. Maybe he was in love with Jeanine, buying her drugs, buying his own.

In Memoriam. Even if it was in neon lights that you were wrong, that you fucked up, you'd be incapable of seeing it, you'd never admit it. You're always right. Don't bother to reply. Eternal disappointment.

What's fifteen miles long and has an asshole on every block? New York's Saint Patrick's Day Parade.

It was awful in. It was more awful out. The sidewalk sellers were out, the sun was high in the sky, it was past noon, the sun was pounding the pavement like a bad cop, beating everyone down. The blankets were littered with condemned bricabrac, dented pots, empty bottles out of medicine cabinets, cracked teapots, the contents of someone's life cobbled together and thrown on a blanket to be sold for quarters. For rent or food or drugs. It was pathetic.

Sweat wet her thighs. She'd get a rash. prickly heat. Everyone was sweating everywhere. The block queen who'd yelled at Roy, I'll eat your ass anytime, honey, was arguing with another blanket merchant. The block queen grabbed a blouse and held it up flamboyantly.

—No one wants this.

He threw the blouse to the ground.

—No one's wearing this style anymore. It's completely out. No
 one's buying it.

He slashed the air in front of him. His scorn for the old style was flagrant.

Paulie was sweating, standing on the corner. He was with Hoover. Last year, the musician who'd given Paulie a home threw a birthday party for Hoover at Brownies, the musty-smelling bar. Posters of Hoover were wheatpasted on buildings around the neighborhood, everyone was invited. When Elizabeth arrived, Hoover was sitting on a barstool, eating some of his presents. Everyone brought him food. The handsome dog was panting, Paulie's skin was copper-colored and leathery from years on the street. Now his toughened skin was streaked with sunburn. He liked being outside even though he had a place to live now.

—It's disgusting, Elizabeth said.

—I'm thirsty all the time.

—Maybe you're rabid.

—Very funny.

—Want a cold drink?

Paulie never had money. She'd never asked him to sit down with her. They'd talked, standing in front of his place, her place, on the corner.

—You buying?

—I'm asking, I'm buying.

—How about the Polish bar?

She should call the room. She didn't. Paulie dropped off Hoover at home. Elizabeth liked interruptions. Interruptions weren't interruptions, nothing was being interrupted, nothing was intended. She didn't want to be in control.

The place was as cool and dark as a fall night. The old man behind the bar said nothing. The beer was cold enough and cheap. Paulie was feeling expansive. They were killing time. It was as perfect as it gets.

—When I went homeless, I was paying a lot of bills I couldn't afford. I wasn't eating properly because of the bills I was paying,
   and I had a feeling I could sort of be a free spirit, and hang out
   with everybody who was hanging out in the neighborhood
   and live outside. I thought I could get by.

—Wish I thought that.

—When you go homeless, you need two things: you need money and you need a bed. I would sleep in a park, before the curfew hit. I would sleep in hallways, I would be invited over to people's houses to sleep, and I always had a good breakfast. The longer I stayed on the street the more hip I became to what was going on. I always had a sketchbook, a pen, and a pencil and I would doodle, carry my books around, and when they became too heavy I would discard them and start over. When Ron took me in I was just beginning to relax on the street. It took me seven years to get back in. Ron did something that not many people would do. He took me in, seeing that I wasn't a bad guy, really, that I was just a little crazy at the time. He said, come on in, pay a little bit of rent, and paint. He put himself out on a limb. I always think about how if it wasn't for Ron I might be still out on the street, or in a hospital, or dead. That's the love relationship that I have with these guys, they treated me better than my parents treated me. They showed me more love than I got at home, that's why I left home. I grew up in a quaint little neighborhood in Brooklyn. A lot of families have kids and the kids suffer because there's nothing for them. I always thought I was artistic, as far back as I can remember. I was always neat and I always wanted things to be beautiful. I always had an eye for things. I would move things around. I was in the living room, and newspapers were scattered around, I would pick up the newspapers and organize them and put them where they belonged.

Elizabeth didn't debate beauty, ugliness, love, or freedom. It was the same argument. There's either too much or too little of any of them.

—I try to make things better. When I first started painting I was involved with negativity, and at a certain point I realized that I wanted to be the kind of artist that would make things better rather than comment on the negative side of things, the ugly side of things. I'm always working on the beautification of the things around me. It's not just me sitting in front of an easel painting a picture. It's getting up in the morning and eating the right food . . .

They ordered another round and some peanuts for Paulie.

—If I make myself healthy and feel good, then I can also make things around me healthy that aren't healthy. I have my breakfast, then I sit in front of my easel and I dream a lot. I just look at what I've done from the day before, or just from the past. I appreciate my work more than I ever did before. If I do something new that makes me happier, I leave my studio, and I socialize a lot after I finish a piece. I really try to be more with the people around me, to just enjoy their company.

Elizabeth was easy, a two-beer drunk. Paulie might be dreaming now. She told him she'd go crazy if she went homeless.

—It helped me straighten out, because I had a lot of time. I didn't work, I had no bills, so I had all this time to think about how things were going for me. I wasn't really happy when I first left home. I left all my old friends because I didn't feel I could fit in. I was always suffering or in pain over one thing or another. When I was on the street I got rid of my shyness, it always got in my way. When I was a kid I couldn't even talk to some people. I had to ask around for small jobs, I had to communicate more with people so I could just get by, and I found that people would give me jobs, or they would give me money free, and say, here's five dollars, get a meal, or invite me in for a shower, a change of clothes. People would invite me in to sleep the night. I slowly became more social . . .

Elizabeth gave him money. She never asked him to come for dinner. She never cooked. Even if she did cook, she wouldn't have. She wasn't Ron.

—You weren't scary and threatening like that hairy, smelly guy on the block last year. He was kind of like a cartoon homeless guy. You didn't know what he was going to do.

—I offered him a sandwich one time, and he said no. I was a cleaning man for the building next to me, and he'd been chased from another stoop, he began to squat on the property I was cleaning. I told him, Listen, if it was up to me, I'd let you stay here. But the tenants, there are children in the building, and there are ladies in the building who are frightened, so you can't stay here. I tried to make that up to him by saying, Do you want a dollar or two? Do you want a sandwich? He'd always say, No, no, no. But I know he was hungry, he would scrounge around in the garbage can for something to eat. I knew he wanted to scare people away.

—You weren't frightening. You were compelling.

Paulie's eyebrows shot up. It was the other-people-are-other-people look.

—A lot of the young people didn't really appreciate my craziness or my living on the street. They would use me as a target for their aggression. They would throw bottles at me and cans, and a couple of times I got into scuffles with people, because I was trying to make things better. I would tell people, Why don't you loosen up a bit? They would take that as an attack on their being, so they would try to chase me, or punch me. I don't recommend leaving home and trying to live on the street at this time. There are too many people who don't appreciate that.

Elizabeth asked Paulie if he meant the crusties.

—I don't understand what they're about. Not that they have to be about anything, but they must have an idea of life that is different from most people. They don't eat that much. I know they drink all the time, and when they're done drinking they leave like fifteen bottles on the street. They break them on purpose. They're interesting to me. They're like gypsies. They're being persecuted. They're constantly moving from block to block to find a place where they can squat and not be told to move.

Elizabeth told him she hated the ground they squatted on.

—I want to have faith in them, and I think they're important to the community because they're a minority which I think should be part of the community and not shunned, pushed aside. Maybe they're sick. I was sick on the street at first. I had my first breakdown, call it a breakdown, in 1967, my friends brought me to a psychiatrist, and he was giving me medication, and that seemed to straighten me out a bit. I wasn't as crazy. But when I moved to our block, in 1971, I began to get

sick again because I wasn't eating right, and it was part of my
illness that I objected to medication, and that was one of the
major keys to my health. It keeps me from hallucinating, getting paranoid.

Paulie was a better person than she was. Elizabeth was
unmedicated.

—Do you remember when we first began to say hello? she asked.

—No, he said.

It was always like that.

—I had a lot of things I was disturbed about. My kid brother died
in Vietnam, and my brother and sister got married and they
moved upstate. They didn't like blacks, or third world com-
munities. Most of my family was like that. When the poor
people, the third world, started to move closer to them, they
decided they didn't want to bring their kids up with that, they
thought it would be a bad influence. They gave up on me too.
My older brother could have taken me in for a while, but there
wasn't room for me. My younger brother was my favorite, and
when he died in Nam, around the same time, my mother was
murdered. She was shot by my stepfather.

His face showed nothing.

—My brother died first. I told him you should try to think twice
before you go in. He didn't, he went and six months later he
died. He got shot down at Hamburger Hill. They took a whole
month to find him. I used to have dreams that he was captured and being tortured. You know, all those stories?

Elizabeth held Paulie's rough hand. Her hand was proofreader
soft.

—He was nineteen, he was gone. My mother got remarried to this guy who was a friend of the family. She was having a hard time with him too. He was a cop, and after he retired, they got a house down in Florida. I didn't see the place, but I can imagine it was terrible. Then all of a sudden we get a phone call, Mom was dead, she was shot by our stepfather. They had a trial in Florida, I was sick, in and out of the hospital. I just couldn't go down to the trial. My family was pissed at me. And revenge hit my family. They wanted to get this guy. My sister was afraid he was going to kill her, she was a little nutty. It wasn't that way. My mother could get under your skin . . .

Elizabeth ordered another round.

—He murdered her, Paulie.

—He killed her, and he got an acquittal.

—On what grounds?

—Florida is kind of a conservative state.

—He didn't do any time?

Elizabeth might not do time for doing a moron. She had more justification. Her action wouldn't be personal. It'd be a social attack.

—My mother was the one who kept the family together, Paulie said.

The bathroom floor was wet. The stall was filthy. No one was hanging from the ceiling, no one was slumped over, dead, on the toilet, with a needle in her arm. The walls were zines.

DUCK LIPS. DUCK LIPS are a girl's best friend.

Duck lips duck lips uber alles.

What can't hurt you can't be much fun. Maxine.

Josie gives great blow jobs.

My cunt is eden.

God is legally blind.

The STAIN...

The stream of hot yellow piss falling from her was satisfying. She was full, now she was emptying herself, it felt good even if it was nothing, and she was an endless river of piss. Elizabeth giggled. Some people believe drinking urine is healthy. People believe anything. She didn't ask Paulie where he shit when he went homeless. She once saw a woman shitting in a phone booth on Wall Street. The cops were there in a second.

Elizabeth called the room from a phone booth next to the bathroom. The room needed her, where was she? Elizabeth heard disappointment in her supervisor's voice. Rose Hill. Rose was the longtime head of the room. Elizabeth couldn't handle the room without Rose. Rose Hill had a life outside the correctional facility. On Fourteenth Street, there was an actual building with her name carved on it.

Paulie went his way, Elizabeth went hers. He waved at her, she waved at him, and then he kept waving, but he didn't turn around, he just waved, his hand flapping behind his back. He kept waving it as he walked farther away. He was already in his world, and she was in hers.

A sandwich walks into a bar and sits down on a barstool. The bartender says, I'm sorry, we don't serve lunch.

A white woman from out of town is staying at a fancy hotel. She gets on the elevator. At the next floor Lionel Ritchie gets on with his dog. The singer commands, Down, down, lie down, to his dog. The woman drops to the floor.

It was a short cab ride, just four avenues west, seven blocks north, walking distance. She was late and high. The driver understood English. He didn't want to talk much. He knew his way. He was tuned to a radio talk show. The talk show host was railing against welfare queens. Taxi drivers turned their radios loud to enflame passengers who were easily driven mad in snarled traffic. There was only one furry deodorant object dangling from his rearview mirror. She tipped him. He didn't say thank you. She slammed the door hard.

She always tipped, except the time she hailed a cab after a late night at work.

—Tompkins Square Park, please.

—You're taking me to the cemetery.

—What'd you say?

—You're taking me to the cemetery.

The cab slowed approaching a red light. Elizabeth opened her door and jumped out. She slammed the door hard. Taxi drivers hated that.

The proofroom was air-conditioned. One of the two obese men, the nicer, funnier one, was there. He didn't sweat much, except for the top of his bald head. Beads of sweat collected there. He had ten fragile hairs, and the sweat flattened those. His bald head was damp and shiny. He was fastidious about his appearance. Roy called him Proofroom Fats.

Proofroom Fats was in an OK mood. When the other obese man wasn't around, he was nicer to Elizabeth.

"Jean-Henri Dunant. 1828-1910. Swiss philanthropist, born in Geneva, inspired the foundation of the International Red Cross after seeing the plight of the wounded on the battlefield of Solferino. His efforts brought about the Conference at Geneva (1863) from which came the Geneva Convention (1854). In 1901, with Frederic Passy, he was awarded the first Nobel Peace Prize."

Gisela was right. It didn't mention his incarceration in a mental hospital. Probably censored by the Swiss government. Everyone else in the room was sullen. The room was correcting articles about the richest people in the world. They read about personal net worth and assets slipping from $2.2 billion to $1.8 billion. She'd been in the room, off and on, more than seven years. She'd cut her proofroom teeth reading about prisons managed by private corporations which profited off prisoners by cutting out desserts, about the parasitic nature of senior citizens, who vote, that's all, so why bother about them, they're just a drain on the economy. The first year was the hardest. She became used to it. Newcomers found it demoralizing.

A snail goes to the police station. He's all beat up. The cop asks who did it. The snail says, a turtle. Can you describe the turtle, the cop asks. How big was he? What color? The snail says, I don't know. It all happened so fast.

After five years, she was allowed to attend the veterans' party. It was in honor of the boss's birthday. Employees were given bonuses equivalent to the years he'd lived plus how many they'd worked for the company. There was a system to the giving that was strictly followed. The boss handed envelopes to all the workers after lunch under a circus tent.

The veterans were transported to the boss's estate by bus.

Two busloads of workers arrived at the estate on a warm morning in September. They were allowed the run of the place, allowed to see the master's bedroom, swim in the pool, play tennis. Elizabeth hung out on the lawn and avoided the main house. She watched the misshapen scene. The servants, the house slaves, served canapes. The house slaves wore white aprons over black uniforms. They scorned the field slaves, the workers brought to the main house as a treat by the master. The house slaves' disdain was painted on their pinched, colorless faces. They held the silver trays painfully far from their bodies, for the field slaves, the lowlife from the city.

Elizabeth didn't eat the cheesy hors d'oeuvres. She talked to people from the room. The proofreaders were scattered uncomfortably over the plush, rolling green lawn. They were unsuitable, not designed for it, eyesores to the house slaves.

One of the boss's sons appeared. The nice, quiet one. He was taking pictures. Without a word, he shot them.

—You didn't ask for my release, Elizabeth said.

—Your release is when you sign the back of your paycheck, he said.

He snapped another picture. He didn't take his eyes from the back of the camera. It took a second, then he realized the naked truth of his words. He became flustered and loped off.

—You could get fired, the nasty obese man warned.

—He doesn't have the courage of his convictions, she said.

Toadies are taking over the world was what she thought.


A man was fucking a girl in the ass. He comes and says, Wasn't that amazing? She says, Actually I found it humiliating. He says, That's a pretty big word for a ten-year-old.


Elizabeth wasn't going to this year's veterans' party. The supervisors weren't happy about it. In a feudal place, employees were expected to show their servile gratitude to the boss.

She worked with her feet on the table of her cubicle, if the editors didn't barge into the room to check up on the misfits, who were in charge of correcting them, which was a joke, and if they did, she read copy with her feet on the floor.

Paulie's mother kept his family together and got murdered by the man she loved. When Paulie went homeless, he got better.

Elizabeth would be here forever for a home and get worse. She was silent, intent upon being silent. She surveyed the room. The readers were concentrating on little black marks on shiny white pages. Doing cold reads.

Elizabeth caught several big mistakes. She corrected them, tidied them up. She was paid for that. She was a superintendent like Hector. But she did her job.

If the errors had gone into the magazine, the room would be in trouble. After the issue appeared, and the offending mistake on the offending page was noticed, it would be copied and sent to the senior editors, maybe even the boss. They'd return copies of the page or pages to the supervisors of the room, and the proofreader would be talked to, and individuals would be warned if it was the second time, fired if they'd been responsible for several mistakes or for one really serious, embarrassing miss that made the company look bad.

A proofreader capped the "t" in a sentence about "tony Bennett College." "Tony Bennett College." He was fired.

That was before Elizabeth arrived.

In time every new reader was told the tale of the proofreader's Tony Bennett error, usually over take-out food. The newcomers learned they could be fired for their errors. The longtimers laughed so hard they couldn't eat. Except for the obese men. They could always eat.

The room parried its futility, fought against its marginality with righteousness. They discussed their endangered work, how no one cared about mistakes in books and newspapers, how editors and especially writers didn't know what they were doing.

—If a carpenter used the wrong tool, he couldn't hang a door properly, Proofroom Fats said.

He was on a roll.

—Always "he," Sally said.

Sally had been in the proofroom the longest.

—There are typos in the *Times'* headlines, Fats went on.

He ignored her.

—*The New York Times* fired all its proofreaders years ago, Sally said.

The room was a den for a dying breed. Nearly extinct. The room corrected errors no one would've noticed. Double quotes inside the period were moved outside the period, different than was changed to different from. The room scorned "between you and I." The correct "me" sounded lower class to people who ached to sound classy. The room understood that all mistakes entered the language after being repeated enough, and someday they'd be correct, so eventually no one writing or speaking would be aware that over time and imperceptibly an array of former misfits had deformed and degraded the language. Language would become garbage. It'd spill out their mouths.

—Language is already garbage, Margaret said.

Margaret was either a meek woman or a snob. She hardly ever spoke. She didn't like Elizabeth's aggressiveness.

They worked in fear. They feared the reduction of their hours, they feared learning they were no longer needed, maybe only one or two of them, they feared becoming redundant. They were skilled workers, too expensive for the company to pay for what everyone knew was unnecessary. They feared being fired.

Some compliments were sent their way. A few. Their work, when it was good, was invisible. The room approached invisibility, like soundtracks in movies. Elizabeth liked movie music.

Two and a half hours later, Elizabeth was released. She made chump change and fulfilled her obligations to the room. She'd keep her objections to language and life to herself.

A man goes hunting for bears. He sees one, takes aim, and just misses. The bullet grazes the bear's shoulder. The bear gets really angry and goes over to the man. He says, you just missed me, you tried to kill me, I'm really pissed at you. I'm going to make you go down on me. So the bear forces the man to go down on him. The man does it. He's chagrined and runs out of the woods. A week later he goes hunting again, finds the bear again, takes really good aim, fires, but misses. The bear's really pissed off. He goes over to the man and forces him to have sex with his arms tied behind him. The man comes back a week later, sees the bear, takes really careful aim, shoots, and misses the bear again. The bear goes over, he's even more pissed off, and he sodomizes the man. The next week the man comes back, takes aim at the bear, and misses again. This time the bear goes over to the man and puts his paws on the man's shoulders. The bear says, This isn't really about hunting, is it?

The sun was lower in the sky, the feeble beginnings of dusk filtered through the dust.

It was less muggy. The start of another weekend. The hitters from Jersey and Queens, the bridge-and-tunnel crowd, were getting ready to flood the neighborhood. Some came running, some came racing in, piled into cars, weekend warriors cruising for pleasure, release, some joy in the commission of small-time crimes. In the summer, on weekend nights it was better to be inside.

Elizabeth knew her route by heart. Any change in her beat was an irregularity, not life-threatening, unless it was.

Imperfect strangers hurried by her. They took up space. They were full of themselves, of piss, like her. They came from disturbed families and controlled hideous feelings which controlled them. Their views of events developed from events and sensations they couldn't remember. Nothing came out in the wash. Everyone performed circus acts of confusion and covered them over like cats cover shit in litter boxes.

Nothing human is unique.

Human beings were walking near her, heading somewhere to something. Life was just around the corner. Without want, their lives would collapse, no one would go anywhere, or do or make anything. Lust marked their hapless faces and misshaped them. They were generally lusterless and misshapen.

Lustful faces gazed anonymously into shop windows or at each other. Lips pursed and relaxed and opened and closed in exasperation and people breathed in and out, heavily, sighing, and they struggled to keep moving. Some walked with a lilt, life was a song they'd written.

Elizabeth reviled the song, pitied the suckers.

An upper-middle-class woman rushed out of a store onto the sidewalk. A little boy about three toddled after her, crying, Mommy, mommy. The woman ignored him and kept walking. He couldn't catch up to her. She pretended to let him, he got closer to her, he stopped crying, and then she raced away again, leaving him alone in the middle of the busy sidewalk. He started crying again, sobbing, Mommy, mommy.

The bewildered little boy nearly fell into the street. Cars skidded and stopped. Mommy walked faster, and the distance lengthened, and the kid grew more hysterical and tripped over his stubby legs, as he tried to keep up and obliterate the violent gap.

—You can't do that to that kid. I'm watching you, Elizabeth shouted.

She turned herself into a stern and forbidding character, an upstanding citizen, even as sweat coated her thighs.

The woman halted in place. She allowed the little boy to catch up to her. Elizabeth watched. The woman took her son's hand. She didn't look at him and she didn't look back at the stern figure who'd threatened, I'm watching you. Mother and son turned a corner and disappeared from sight. The woman would beat him later, at home. She wouldn't be surveilled by a City agency.

Elizabeth liked the role, vigilante, citizen executioner. She wanted to arrest the mother. She thought she should. They were enough like each other for her to yell at the woman without fear of the woman's coming after her. She was able to intimidate her. She had to seize any opportunity she could.

What do you call one white guy with two black guys?
A victim.

What do you call one white guy with twenty black guys?
Coach.

What do you call one white guy with two thousand black guys?
Warden.

What do you call one white guy with 200,000 black guys?
Postmaster General.

It was not the best of times, it was not the worst of times. Comparisons were stupid. Reason was history.

Elizabeth breathed automatically. Her past and future gasped together. She exhaled a current of air, time, The atmosphere was a weight on everyone. Thick, wet air contained the city.

—If it's the end, you might be relieved, one guy said to another.

They were walking in front of her, fusion candidates for a new order, a threat to the visible old order. They broke one mold, established another. They might become research scientists or rob banks. No one would be able to describe them accurately for a police drawing.

—He might've been Caucasian with some Asian, or African with some Puerto Rican and Chinese, I don't know, part Indian maybe, too.

The boys laughed raucously. Nothing permanent could ever happen to them. It was a feeling she remembered.

Elizabeth had another feeling now, a sensation, a close feeling, something was close, too near like a bad dream below the surface. It might just be the closeness of the young night forcing itself upon her after hours of airless air-conditioning. She crossed streets several times as she walked closer to her block.

Sometimes she varied her route, just to vary it. Sometimes she crossed the street to avoid an encounter, sometimes she crossed the street because she thought she was being followed. She crossed the street to avoid an encounter with the Korean florist. The Korean florist ran out to the sidewalk anyway and waved wildly. He usually did when he saw her, especially when his wife wasn't in the shop. Elizabeth didn't go into the store much, ever since the florist had taken her hand, when his wife wasn't there, faced her, and stated solemnly, I love you.

He was new to the neighborhood. His English wasn't good. She gave him the benefit of the doubt. He might've meant it in a different way, but she didn't go into his shop much anymore. Passing it was a problem. He knew she wasn't going to buy flowers from him. He was disappointed, he was resigned. She didn't return his love.

Korean florists were usually part of a Korean grocery store. This man was on his own, a maverick, an outcast from the immigrant Korean community. He had a small shop with the usual and limited number of flowers. He was a disgrace, scorned by his native community. As he sucked on his cigarette and stared at the sidewalk, he was figuring how to outfox his enemies. Maybe he thought if Elizabeth loved him and married him, he'd be all right, he'd get a green card, they couldn't get him.

Elizabeth avoided him and entered the pasta store.

—Ciao, bella, the pasta man said.

The pasta man made fresh pasta and mozzarella, and he cured olives, in his other store in Brooklyn. He or his son brought the food to the block six days a week.

The pasta man cut a chunk of parmesan cheese. He bagged a pound of multicolored fettuccini for a German guy with bleached blond hair. The guy paid. The pasta man nodded conspiratorially at Elizabeth when the door shut after the German.

—I worked in Germany, in a factory, because my brother was an engineer, and he says, Come, come, you make more money in Germany, so I did, for three years, I go, but I no like it. No, Germany, no, factory. It's not . . .

He pointed around the store.

—Pasta is my life. Pasta and focaccia and sun-dried tomatoes.

It's what I love.

The pasta man was an inspiration to her and the block.

Elizabeth bought a carton of milk from the corner bodega. Run by Syrians. A familiarly strange man brushed against her as she entered. He glanced at her. She glanced at him. He was the kind of guy she might've fucked years ago. He was a certain type, and for that type, she was a certain type. There's an instant attraction, unquestioned, and there's hardly any bother. Before AIDS, you'd fuck.

Three teenaged boys were at the counter. Two bought potato chips, the third couldn't decide. He wavered, swaying stoned in front of the ice cream freezer. He held up the line. The Syrian owner was patient, Elizabeth wasn't.

—Do you know what you want? Elizabeth asked.

—I want a woman. Wanna jump my bones?

The teenager leered at her lopsidedly.

—I'm too old for you, she said.

She didn't believe that. Lust didn't wither with age. Maybe he thought she was a working girl. The boys snickered.

She studied him. He was a kid and he was talking up for skeletal sex, for boning, moaning, raplike sex, not rapture, maybe rapture. Duck lips uber alles, ducks don't have lips, no bones about it, no flesh, no sins of the flesh. He's not cute enough.

—I don't want to jump your bones, Elizabeth said.

The boy looked shocked, knocked back into a littler place. The Syrian grocer didn't smile or laugh. The exchange may have been objectionable to him. But he'd heard and seen worse since he left Syria. His bodega was on the corner where Jeanine worked.

His brother had dropped to the bottom of the drug well. His brother must've tried the stuff one night, maybe the first time he was given it free, a taste, so he wouldn't chase the dealers from the corner, territory that was always being negotiated, and then he did the stuff again, and more, and had to pay, and did more and more, and then she didn't see him in the store, she saw him on the corner, she saw him wasting away, becoming weightless, becoming angrier, arguing with himself. Then she didn't see him at all.

There are a couple of white guys in Africa. They're captured by remote tribe. The chief says, You have two choices, Death or Ru Ru. The first guy says, Well, death's kind of final. So I guess I'll take Ru Ru. The Chief turns around to his 150 best warriors and he calls out, Ru Ru. The warriors line up and each one sodomizes the guy, until he's a bloody mess and dies. The Chief goes up to the next guy and says, Death or Ru Ru? So the guy says, I guess I'll take death. The Chief turns to his warriors and says, Death . . . by Ru Ru.

The young Korean woman at the dry cleaners had elaborately painted fake nails. They didn't interfere with her picking up dry cleaning slips, writing them and handing customers their cleaning.

The young woman frowned as she handed Elizabeth her cleaning. She was ordinarily oppressively happy, especially after she'd gone shopping and found something great. But her previous customer had accused her of deliberately destroying his best suit.

—He's paranoid, Elizabeth said.

—I don't care he's annoyed. . .

—Par-a-noid . . .

—Whatever, he shouldn't talk to me like that.

Elizabeth left, carrying pasta, bread, milk, and a long and heavy bag of cleaning encased in plastic. It touched the ground. She felt burdened.

Everyone was hanging out, expecting a cooler night.

A grizzled waste of a man, around sixty, ambled toward her, he nearly collapsed, then raised himself up and hit into her, hit hard against her, bounced off her, and grunted. He produced other guttural sounds. His trousers were down around his thighs. He was blind drunk. A young Hispanic guy was chasing after him. He had a ring in his ear.

—Fucking pervert, fucking pervert! he yelled.

The Hispanic guy stopped. He was enraged, steaming. He rubbed the ring in his ear.

—What's up? Elizabeth asked.

—The fucking pervert was taking his pants down in front of the kids—FUCKING PERVERT—I can't stand that shit.

—The Boys Club?

—He's going up to the kids and saying, Want to see a big one? A real big one? FUCKING PERVERT!

The Hispanic guy kept looking down Avenue A and yelling at the drunk. The old man was laughing, holding his trousers with his hands, rambling and hitting into other people.

—I fucking hate those guys.

The Hispanic guy spit. He strutted in circles. Neck straining, veins popping, bug-eyed with furry, he watched the drunken man. Elizabeth watched with him. Nothing to do. They both walked away.

She wondered how many men were exposing their penises to kids, at any one time in the Western world, the part that was awake when she was.

A man goes to his doctor. The doctor looks grim and says the tests have come back. There are two pieces of bad news. You have cancer and you have Alzheimer's. The guy's stunned. He says, I have cancer. But at least I don't have Alzheimer's.

The shit was still in the vestibule. It had hardened. The stench permeated the small space. A junkie in a suit was on the floor. He was winding a tie around his arm. She startled him. He looked up. She frowned. He quickly started unwinding the tie. She looked down at him with disgust. Her lips curled.

—That's it, Elizabeth said.

—I'm sorry, I'm going, he said.

He was a middle-class junkie, probably just off work, scored on the corner. A weekend habit.

—I've had it, Elizabeth said.

—I'm sorry, I'm going. Don't call the cops.

—It's not just you.

—I'm sorry, I'm going. I apologize.

He scurried off. He didn't look back and tidied himself running. He straightened his jacket.

Perverts and weekend junkies and weekend warriors and useless Hector and the room and a pile of dried-up, stinking shit.

Elizabeth tramped up the filthy stairs. A tenant had torn down her sign asking everyone not to put their cigarettes out on the floor.

The tape was still there. Some tenants didn't deserve a place to live. She bent down and picked up a pack of matches some slob had thrown on the stairs.

Elizabeth reached her landing. She didn't look down, she stepped down. She stepped on the plastic bag covering the drycleaning. She slid forward and hit her head on Oscar's doorknob. Hit it hard. She fell to the floor and landed on her knee. Her knee crushed the carton of milk she was carrying.

She was knocked silly. Finally she raised herself up, holding onto the doorknob. She searched for her keys, opened her door, and, rubbing her head, went to the sink to find a sponge to clean up the milk.

There was almost no milk on the landing. Nothing on the floor, except a few drops of milk and the nearly empty carton. She stood there.

A door opened downstairs. The Lopezes' grandmother came out. She'd heard the crash against the door.

—Lizbet? You are there?

—I fell down. On my milk. Don't worry. I'm OK.

—Something's dripping here, Mrs. Lopez said.

She didn't want to explain it to Mrs. Lopez. There was no trace of the milk. There was some milk dripping downstairs. There was no place to go but down.

Dazed, she noticed the wide gap under Oscar's door. The door was set incorrectly. The tenement building, with age, had shifted drastically. The floors weren't level. They were so uneven Elizabeth had to shove a thick shimmy under the file cabinet, otherwise the drawers would slide out. Their weight could topple the cabinet.

A heavy, metal drawer could hit you in the head as you walked by. A file cabinet, dead weight, falling on you could crush you to death.

The milk had flowed under Oscar's door, into his apartment. Elizabeth knocked. He wasn't home. She phoned him, left a message.

—This is Elizabeth, from next door. When you come home tonight, you'll see some milk on your floor near your door—I hope it's not curdled—that's mine. I fell on my milk carton after I slid on my dry cleaning and hit my head against your door. I'm sorry. 'Bye.

Elizabeth put on a CD, the soundtrack from *Taxi Driver*, and sat down at the rectangular table in the kitchen. It was hotter inside than out.

There was a note from Ernest. He'd slid it under the door the way he'd done the first time he'd contacted her, to fight the increase.

*Dear Elizabeth,*

*If you're around I'd like to discuss the latest—strange woman vomiting on third floor; and who's got the boiler key now that Hector's in disgrace; and of course this door problem, defecation in the vestibule; also someone taking dumps on the roof. Landlord, claims he will switch intercom to outside and give us a new locked outside door in two weeks. Do we believe this?*

*See you. Ernest*

Hector's in disgrace?

There was a form letter from Gloria. It was a City regulation that if tenants had kids under the age of ten, they were required to have guards on their windows. Children ten and under were legally protected from falling out windows. Children over the age of ten, who cares.

"Elizabeth Hall, you've won a million dollars. You only have to phone us to get your prize."

"When decisions are made before death, everyone can have input." Larry had sent her name to a cemetery in Queens, to receive its monthly newsletter. He got it too.

Elizabeth opened the pack of matchless matches she'd picked up. There was a handwritten message on the inside cover:

YOU, LOWLIFE DIRTY LITTLE PERVET PEEP HOLE BIG LOUSY SCUM SUCIN NOSE HOW BAG BUTT FUCKTN BEEF BOY! What's your phone #?

A cop left a message on her answering machine. He couldn't have been paying attention.

—Mark, this is Sergeant O'Hara calling from work. Your work vacation—you still got it, but your assignment's been changed—give me a call tomorrow, Saturday, during the second platoon. I'll be in working. 'Bye.

He might be the one who said he was sending cars when they never showed Up. Maybe he thought he'd sent them.

Messages from Larry, Helen, one freelance job, one party, and one plaintive wail from Greta. Regreta.

I have to tell her, end it.

Then the breather. He left heavy breathing messages. He couldn't experience her response. It didn't figure even as a perversion.

Roy came through the door. Fatboy was excited.

—You staying in tonight?

—Watching the game.

—Me too.

—You have eyes for Chinese or BBQ?

—BBQ

—Beer?

—I had some beers with Paulie.

—Street Paulie?

—His mother was murdered, and his brother died in Nam.

—No kidding.

—Paulie's stepfather did it.

—Yeah? The Confidence Game's finished. It's shit.

Roy wrote computer software.

—Don't mention shit.

Roy sniffed sarcastically.

—I went to the room.

—Did Proofroom Fats pop you?

—Why?

—Your forehead's black and blue.

She looked in the mirror, then told Roy about sliding on the dry cleaning and falling on the milk carton.

—What if Oscar slides on the milk when he gets home? Roy asked.

Roy laughed in the shower. When he came out, wrapped in a towel, light brown hairs were stuck to his wet, white legs and chest. She liked his body. She didn't know if it was because it was him or not.

—You like me because I make you laugh, she said.

—I prefer that, he said.

—To what?

—To the alternative.

—Want to have sex?

Even a familiar body was different. It was never safe. Sex was an acceptable risk most people took. It wasn't acceptable, it was uncontrollable. She was part of Roy's fantasy life, it was terrifying. It was frustrating when she couldn't score her own fantasy. Be her own fantasy. If she tried too much, she couldn't get into the sex, because she wasn't concentrating on what was under her hands or on top of her. She had the same mind scripted in her cells, it didn't turn out new material. She wanted to be hot and cold, icy fingers stroking her overheated body, men frozen erect in stupefaction, husky men and furry dogs with long pink tongues. Alaska, maybe. That wasn't her fantasy. The dumb show of hands, tongue, penis prevailed. A perfume, surrender, overtook her, surprised her. Her flesh sometimes failed her, mostly didn't. Roy didn't fail her.

—aaah—

If she wasn't having sex, the sounds of sex were exciting or annoying.

The Pope arrives at Kennedy Airport. He's late for a speech at the UN. He gets into a cab and asks the driver to drive as fast as he can to the UN. The driver's afraid he'll get a ticket, so he doesn't drive fast enough. The Pope's annoyed. The driver says, You're the Pope, you drive, they won't give you a ticket. So the Pope gets in the driver's seat, and the driver gets in back. The Pope floors the car. But a police car stops them and pulls them over. The cop goes over to the car, takes out his pad, and looks in. He sees the driver and phones his precinct. The cop says, I think I just made a big mistake. I pulled over a car for speeding. I don't know who's in the back seat, but the Pope's driving.

Last night Roy and Elizabeth were watching TV. In a commercial, a woman and man were about to have sex or just had sex. He comes to her from behind, drapes a silk robe around her shoulders, and nuzzles the back of her neck.

—You never do that to me, Elizabeth said.

—We've never been in a commercial together, Roy said.

No one obliterates the rage and empty craziness that ignites want. Your release is dressed up as pleasure, and it relentlessly tries to limit its damage and change its image.

Your soundcheck is in the mail, one musician said to another.

What's the first thing you do when you see a spaceman?
You park, man.

Her need was ugly to her, a salivating, gaping mouth. Commercials addressed the sloppy void, and Elizabeth liked commercials. They were anti-death. You had to be alive to buy things.

Elizabeth heard the orgasms of the women below. They could hear hers. The tenants acted as if they didn't hear anything, as if they lived in soundproof boxes, otherwise being in close quarters couldn't work. Thin walls make bad neighbors.

Tenants pretended to be deaf and blind to each other. For sounds like orgasms and fights, acknowledgment was taboo.

Cool orgasm you had last night.

That fight about washing the dishes—when you threw the dishes on the floor—incredible.

Music volume was something else. There was a rock musician who used to live above her. His band started practicing at 2 A.M.

The guy was stoned when Elizabeth appeared in a robe at his door at 3 A.M.

—This has got to stop, she said.

—Is this waking you? he asked.

He asked his question at the door with a roomful of musicians behind him, and all of them had to turn down so he could hear himself and her response. A microphone was plastered to a woman's open mouth. Stacks of black equipment were mounted everywhere. The gaggle of musicians gaped at the sleep-deprived female intruder.

—Your drummer's playing a full drum kit, you're all amplified, you're right above me, and you're asking me if this is waking me? Are you out of your mind?

He was too lamebrained to respond, too drugged-out.

Now, she concentrated on the matter at hand and the matter in her. Elizabeth came, Roy came. Roy always delivered. Then he turned on his computer. He entered cyberspace where no one knew his name.

BBQ didn't deliver. She'd pick up dinner tonight, she felt more generous after sex. She switched on News Channel 4. Al Roker. Sue Simmons. News was nothing without them.

Everything was as stupid and smart as the best show on TV. TV was a plain place, a plain face. People trusted a plain face.

TV voices were sonorous, electromagnetic. TV was a habit and a bunch of regular guys, always available. She was a TV baby and TV was home away from home at home.

People want the facts, the news, fantasies were news, facts were fantasies. All fantasies were true, all news was good news, no news was bad news. A father beat his child to death, a dog found its way home, a country has a famine. Everyone wants some excitement, but not too much. No one wants to have to leave home, no one has to, TV's a domestic animal. Elizabeth's appetite for food, news, disaster, gossip was healthy or unhealthy. She adjusted to disasters, watched them become less alarming over time. The unusual mutated into the usual. The grotesque was homey. They sent in the serious news clowns when things were really bad.

O. J. Simpson had been charged for the murders of his exwife and her friend. New York was charged up for the Knicks game. It was an OK news night.

Elizabeth walked down the dirty stairs and out the disgusting vestibule. Fatboy was with her on a leash. He slowed her up, sniffing and pissing. Everyone's less threatening with a dog, unless it's a pit bull.

The street was holding its collective breath. We won't breathe until the night says yes. Humidity hung in the at, dampening Elizabeth's low spirits. People were getting off work sporting a weekend mentality. Others were working, dealing, others were buying their good time.

A man who lived in New York City couldn't stand it anymore. So he moved to Montana. His closest neighbor was ten miles away.

The first month was great—he didn't see anyone. It was quiet. After three months he started to get restless. After six months he was so bored, he thought about moving back to the city. A neighbor called. He invited him to a party. The neighbor said, Get ready for a lot of drinking, fighting, and fucking. Great, the man said. Who'll be there? You and me, the neighbor said.

Hector shot a jaundiced eye in her direction. He tipped his hat. It inspired the usual panic. His courteous gesture was meant to obscure his hatred of her. All gestures disguised something worse.

Hector's in disgrace.

Maybe he was humiliated by the Big G, maybe she used her big mouth to tear him down in front of his wife. Maybe he'd take his revenge like one of those postal workers who returns a week after being fired with an AK-47 and slaughters his former boss and five colleagues. Walking into any post office, arguing in a post office, was tinged with the possibility of a civil service employee going berserk.

Elizabeth didn't want to be in Hector's line of fire when he went psycho. She'd complained about the halls, Gloria had opened her big mouth to him, compromised her, and now he's in disgrace. TENANT MURDERED BY DISGRACED SUPER.

The acerbic super waved her over.

—Did you see that filth Jeanine in the doorway last night?

—I don't think . . .

—She was giving a blow job right out there in a doorway. She's filth.

—She's OK.

—She's an animal.

179

The acerbic super sneered. He thought everyone was an animal. He cleaned up after people. He bagged garbage and placed covers on garbage cans. During the snowstorm of 1993, no garbage was collected for days. The acerbic super bagged and rebagged garbage, tried to keep his sidewalk clear, hosed the blackened snow away with hot water. Late at night, homeless and poor people scavenged and tore the bags apart and spilled the trash over the sidewalk. The acerbic super had to bag it all again.

She didn't blame him for being pissed off.

Some scavengers didn't tear bags apart. Some searched through the garbage and retied the bags. Most didn't. Supers were responsible to landlords and landlords to the City for the careless actions of the desperate who didn't give a kissless fuck about the block. They were hungry, scrounging for scraps, and everyone acknowledged that and blamed them without furry. The acerbic super had to clean up after them. He hated them.

Paulie was home with Hoover. They lived in a storefront, behind a window to the street. Elizabeth could always see in. They could see her seeing in. Hoover was lying on his side, his legs apart. He wasn't panting. Some Filipinos were congregating in the new Filipino-owned cafe. The West Indian guys were loading out for a gig. They'd been busted some nights ago. Everyone was back.

Jeanine was on the corner. Weekend busy. The other drug runners noticed Elizabeth and Jeanine, took the scene in, no hostile comments or looks. One of them petted Fatboy. Fatboy rolled over and spread his legs obscenely.

—You see this, Liz, people getting high on the block. The boss doesn't want it, so we don't get high on the block, but the customers come and they're so desperate, they'll smoke on the block. They'll just pull it in the doorway and take a crack pipe and smoke the crack in the door, and that's not right. We argue with them, tell them to get off the block. It scares people walking down the street. They know us, but they see people they don't know, and it scares them. It's bad for us 'cause it's like always our fault. That's what's probably bringing the cops down on us a lot too.

The boss was right. Elizabeth didn't want a weekend warrior on crack lunging at her from a doorway. Jeanine's mother was threatening to throw her out again.

—It's your mother's dementia...

—The AIDS, and she's crazy to begin with. She gets high, and either she blames me—number one—for what's going on her in life, or she sits and feels sorry for what she's done to my life. She sits there and cries...

Jeanine glanced behind her nervously.

—I gotta do something besides sell drugs. I keep going to jail.

Jeanine's gray-green eyes were lit by a thousand points of artificial light. She'd straightened her hair again. She couldn't stop moving. Her gelled hair lay still as a grave on her head as she treaded sidewalk. Jeanine fast-talked Elizabeth. Fatboy strained on his leash.

—I don't have my children, I don't have anything. So when my mother dies—not that I have really anything, but when she dies I'll have nothing. My sister and I are on and off the lease whenever her dementia sets in. I have to do something with my life, I have to go back to school. I gotta do something besides sell drugs...

Jeanine might sell drugs until she dropped. They both knew that. They talked about change. It was a version of the conversation she had with friends. Elizabeth was going to quit her job, stop doing something, love and work were everything, nothing, there were no men, no jobs, there was no sex, nothing to live or die for, and if there wasn't anything, anyone, to want or support you, why bother, because it was hard to change, and most change was small change.

I might not make it back to this corner, Elizabeth thought as she left it.

Two African-American men fly to Africa for a vacation. They get off the plane and hear drumming. The drumming goes on night and day. They ask people, Why is there drumming all the time? People say, Drum stop, very bad, very bad. The drums continue, all the time, night and day. Then, one day, suddenly, the drums stop. The men ask everyone, What's going on? What's happening? Everyone says, It's very bad, very bad. They keep asking, But why's it bad? What's so bad? Finally an old man says, Drums stop, bass solo.

The Dallas BBQ restaurant was Friday-night alive and air-conditioned to death. Video wall screens were a distraction when you had nothing to say. The room was loud, filled with echoes, like a public swimming pool, with people shouting for help from waiters, sound bouncing off the walls, an acoustical nightmare. Black and white people ate together and at separate tables. Barbecue and soul food integrated New York, nothing else, not clubs, not schools, not music.

—A whole chicken, one piece of corn bread, cole slaw, two
baked potatoes.

—Is that all?

—Yeah.

—You got it.

The BBQ eaters, oblivious of other tables, of Elizabeth, were
gulping beer from frosted mugs. Her eyes traveled from table to
table of people out for a good time, the pursuit of a good time was
pathetic. BBQ was a cheap good time.

People were weird eating, weird with their noses and mouths and
dead cells jutting from ends of frantic fingers grasping at straws and
chicken body parts, weird whether they chewed with their mouths
open or shut.

Her eyes nearly finished circling the room, then she saw
Vomithead, Vomithead's son and daughter, and Vomithead's mother.

They're alive, she thought.

Elizabeth collided with herself, with an obstacle lodged in her. She
fell back against the stiff chair. The quartet appeared not to see her.
She waited for her number to be called. The floor could cave in and
they could drop through a hole and never be found. A bomb could be
planted by a white supremacist. It could explode right after Elizabeth
left, blithely carrying away her whole chicken and cole slaw.

Vomithead's betrayal couldn't be undone or forgotten.

Elizabeth prepared her speech, rehearsed. She'd walk over,
ignore the mother, who was beneath contempt, and the son and
daughter, who were products of an otherwise unproductive woman,
and glare at, but not into, her ex-friend's familiar deceptive eyes and
ask: Why aren't you dead?

That wasn't sufficient.

A priest, a pastor, and a rabbi play golf every week. One weekend they're behind a golfing party that's very slow. It's holding up their game and they're not having any fun. They go to the groundskeeper and say, What's going on? The groundskeeper tells them it's a party of blind golfers. The priest says, I'm so ashamed of myself, it's part of the Church's teaching to have patience. The pastor says, And I too preach tolerance every Sunday. The rabbi says, yes, I do too, but why can't they play at night?

Her order arrived, her number was called. Maybe it wasn't Vomithead. Elizabeth wouldn't be able to recognize her anyway. She hadn't recognized her when she knew her. Vomithead could've shifted into another set of chickenshit body parts. Elizabeth didn't glance her way again.

If she thought about someone enough, that person appeared on the next block, like a horror movie.

BBQ was tainted now. Another place was spoiled. Miscreants from yesterday slimed into today. Spoilers were everywhere, thriving on their own misery, making other people miserable. Some of them, like Vomithead, had children to make miserable.

The older you grew, if you grew older, the more people you didn't say hello to, the more people you avoided. The living dead cluttered the route. Men she'd fucked years ago walked into crummy coffee shops and sat down next to her. Friends she'd once trusted were specters who entered bitterly into neutral corridors and destroyed the spirit in them. It wasn't hard to make friends, it was easy. Friends don't sign contracts. It's why friendships weren't taken seriously and marriage was. Life is littered with broken friendships.

Elizabeth took the long way home and avoided the corner. An elderly white man was behind her, muttering to himself.

—Fuck them, fuck them, fuck them.

Elizabeth slowed down. He came closer.

—Fuck them, fuck them, fuck them, Hitler was right.

The elderly white man was shabby and unshaved. He wheeled around in circles and searched the street for evidence of his enemies.

—Fuck them, fuck them, Hitler was right.

Elizabeth slowed down even more. She was next to him. He stopped talking out loud. He'd violated her mental space, she mentally engaged him in conversation.

Why don't you join a militia so you can go kill some blacks and Jews and take over the government?

He probably believed in God.

You really think Hitler would save you?

Militias were worse than the junkies in her vestibule. Junkies weren't sanctimonious. They knew they were worthless assholes.

Elizabeth guarded her life. She frowned and set her mouth into an angry trap, then kept her trap shut.

In Memoriam. Life's stupid and the same as when you left. Tell me what death's like. Light and tunnel? Bridge and tunnel here. Miss you.

What's the difference between meat and chicken?

If you beat your chicken, it dies.

Hector wasn't in front of the building. Gone. probably setting a fire in the basement.

On the stairs near her apartment, she was blocked by a drunk hulk. Probably one of the people who camped at Ernest's door.

. . . sad-looking woman descending with her bedding late last night. . . strange man outside my door coughing. . . feel like I'm a denizen of Devil's Island.

Elizabeth gripped her keys. Her fingers were white and red around them. She always took her keys out a block ahead of home. She had four of them on a chain and placed one between each finger. Then she made a fist. The keys jutted out from her fist. If she was attacked, she'd rip the man's skin with the keys' sharp edges, rip his face to shreds. She had her keys splayed, ready.

The hulk had inflamed skin, enlarged pores. He stank. Maybe he had TB. She didn't want to breathe his air. He was probably the guy Roy checked out on the stairs last night, the guy refusing to give an inch. Why should he.

Now she could barely squeeze past him. Their bodies touched regrettably. He was fierce and silent. He didn't bother to look up at her. He was probably the one taking dumps on the roof.

What are the three reasons we know Jesus was Jewish?
1. Because he lived at home until he was thirty-three.
2. Because he thought his mother was a virgin.
3. Because his mother thought he was God.

Roy was home. If she was alone, about to be a prisoner in her apartment, she called the cops. She used to give creeps the benefit of the doubt. They were menacing, she ignored them. They squatted at her door, she played live-and-let-live, and paced back and forth in her apartment until they left.

The last time the cops arrived, the man had vanished. He'd left his greasy gear. The cops put on rubber gloves, bagged it and threw it on the street.

One of the cops was sexy. He looked into her apartment when she opened the door. Roy warned, never let cops inside. She wanted him to come in. She'd never been attracted to a cop before, except on TV. It was inevitable she'd fall in love with one for a minute. She was thrown into contact with them. She'd even had a police escort, because of a murder across the street.

It was balmy that night. The rookie cop lifted the yellow tape for her to walk under. Her building was technically in the crime scene.

—Where's Dennis Franz? Where's Detective Sipowicz? Elizabeth asked the cop.

Without missing a beat, the cop motioned across the street to the drug store where the dealer had been murdered.

—That's our Sipowicz, he said.

The guy he pointed to didn't look anything like the TV character. It didn't matter. Thousands of movies, TV shows, and commercials were shot in the neighborhood, it was an inner-city set. "NYPD Blue" was special, because it used the facade of the local station house. Sipowicz, or Dennis Franz, was a cop with a pockmarked human face. He was the plain face of TV.

Sipowicz once told his fiance, a DA, about a grisly murder, when a dog ate a baby murdered by its mother. Sipowicz had to cut open the dog's stomach, so he was the one who discovered the baby in pieces. Sipowicz's pain is in the pauses. He tells his fiance that the priest who's going to marry them "asked me if I lost my faith." Long, soulful pause. Then he says, quietly, "I got faith in you." It doesn't count that on "Hill Street Blues" Dennis Franz played a creep. All that's in the past.

The night of the murder across the street, the yellow tape marking off the perimeter of the crime scene waved in the breeze for hours. Uniforms and detectives hung out drinking coffee until it was light. Elizabeth didn't leave her window until they tore down the tape and drove away. It was like TV except she couldn't hear the dialogue.

Everyone was a hostage to something.

She was thrown together with cops. It was inevitable that she'd fall in love with one, that she'd want a cop to invade her space, be her private dick, her space invader, for one New York minute.

Birds do it,
bees do it,
even people with Tourette's
FUCK
do it

Now Elizabeth set the BBQ chicken down on the stack table near the TV, with plates and forks, and opened the hot aluminum-lined bags. She threw away the plasticware, which could break into pieces as you chewed. Shards of plastic could lodge in your throat. She had a strategy for choking alone. She'd hurl herself against a hardbacked chair and perform a self-Heimlich maneuver.

Roy was watching "The Simpsons."

—There's a man in the hallway, she said.

—Yeah?

—He stinks.

—Who doesn't.

Elizabeth forgot about Vomithead and Hector. After a while, she forgot about the drunk hulk in the hallway. She knew he could hear every sound in their apartment. He was probably leaning against their wall, listening to the Knicks game.

A ventriloquist's act is going nowhere. He's competing with TV and movies, he's lost his audience. His agent comes to him and says, Listen, I can't represent you anymore. No one's booking you. You're going to have to find a new line of work. So the ventriloquist opens a store. It's called Speak to Your Dead Relatives. The first day a woman comes in and says, I'd like to speak to my dead husband. The ventriloquist says, That'll be one hundred dollars. Then she says, And I'd like him to speak to me. The ventriloquist says, That'll be two hundred dollars. And, he adds, if he speaks to you while I'm swallowing a glass of water, that'll be three hundred dollars.

During a commercial Elizabeth poured a beer and went to the window. A lot of people had the game on. Small windows glowed inside big windows. she looked down. The street was empty.

—Come here, look at this, Roy said.

A white car on a highway crossed the screen. The Knicks game was interrupted by a newsman's voice. A white car was driving alone on a six-lane highway.

—Weird, Roy said.

The game was being interrupted. Elizabeth knew interruptions were life. Nine black-and-white police cars were following a white car, a Bronco, and they were in formation, keeping their distance. O. J. Simpson's inside, an announcer said. His ex-wife, Nicole, and her male friend, Ron Goldman, were murdered last week. O.J.'s under arrest for the murders. He's got a gun to his head. His best friend, A.C. Cowlings, is driving, speaking to the cops on a car phone. O.J.'s going to kill himself.

Roy and Elizabeth watched the game and the car. The Knicks were beating the Rockets. O.J. couldn't turn himself over to the cops. He wanted to see his mother. Patrick Ewing was sweating, drenched. A.C. kept talking to the cops on the car phone. O.J. wanted to go to his mother, to his home or to the cemetery, to Nicole's grave. Starks missed a basket. Elizabeth started to cry.

—What's the matter? Roy asked. The Knicks are winning.

If he did it, anyone could do it. No one was safe from each other or from themselves. He wants to go home to his mother.

—I just saw him in *Naked Gun 33 1/2*. He was funny, she said.

—The first *Naked Gun* was funnier.

Elizabeth walked to the window. The white car was traveling on the highway across most of the green screens.

Helen phoned.

—They're waving to him, she said.

—The cars are parked on the highway. . .

—I love live TV.

—Me too.

Helen walked fast and didn't stand and talk in doorways, which drove Elizabeth crazy. Helen got to the point and didn't turn life's puny moments into rites of passage. She didn't make cruel and unusual demands. Elizabeth hoped it would last. Helen drove a school bus for a private school. Her psychiatrist parents felt they'd raised a failure. Helen told them it was better than dancing naked on top of a bar.

—What're you going to do? Helen asked.

—Nothing. Are you going anywhere?

—Nowhere fast.

They always said that.

The car turned into O.J.'s driveway. Cowlings parked it at the front door. Cowlings got out, O.J. was hidden, there was confusion, Cowlings talked with some police, finally O.J. emerged. He surrendered.

How do you know when a cop is dead?

The doughnut falls out of his hand.

The Knicks won by seven points. Heavenly screams of basketball joy rang down the block. Some morons had congregated on the church steps. The news kept showing clips of another friend of O.J.'s reading O.J.'s suicide letter. Elizabeth had another beer. She studied the morons. They looked like the ones from last night. Some of the Pick Me Up crusties were with them.

—Get away from the window, Roy said.

—No.

—You're going to get killed.

—So what.

Elizabeth thought about murder, about dying, throat slashed, blood gushing.

—When you're old, and your friends start dying all around you, don't you think that'll be hard?

—It depends on whether they owe me money or not, Roy said.

If O.J. could do it, anyone could do it. Husbands murder their wives, ex-wives all the time. They murder them in courtroom hearings about protection orders against them.

All the TVs across the street showed the white Bronco and the cop cars in formation, reruns of his run from the cops.

She didn't want to do time for doing a moron. Murdering someone you loved made more sense. In a flaming instant of furious, senseless passion, she could stab Roy in his heart. Then he'd be dead. It was too final. All she wanted was to hurt him, teach him a lesson. If she could imagine it, it didn't mean she could do it, it was just within reach, in the realm of possibility, which was important, because as you got older, you felt more limited.

There was a sharp knock at the door.

Roy was in cyberspace.

It was Ernest.

—Hector's been fired, he said.

—What'd he do? Why was he in disgrace?

—I don't know. But it must have been really bad, because we have no super.

Ernest came in, and they sat down at the rectangular kitchen table. Elizabeth opened some beers. She wasn't in love with him anymore. They had a lot in common.

—We have no super. What if something happens? she asked.

—We'll call the landlord's office.

—At night?

—I don't know.

—Are they going to hire a new super?

—They'll try to rent Hector's apartment for big bucks.

—They'll have to get his stuff out.

—That could take a year.

They emptied their glasses. Elizabeth sighed and opened more bottles.

—What if the electricity goes out at midnight? she asked.

—I don't know.

—What if the boiler explodes at 3 A.M.?

—We're dead.

—Hector was better than nothing.

—We'll have to contact the City.

—In the middle of the night?

—If it's an emergency, we'll call the fire department or the cops. What else can we do?

I don't want to be sorry to lose a super like Hector. I want to be free of Hector and the cops, she thought.

—You know, the cops never get right on it, Elizabeth said.

—Yeah, they're hanging out or practicing cop triage. I saw this rookie at the corner today, and both of us were standing near this crazy, he's wearing farmer overalls, a tall, skinny loony dude, with a real long gray beard, a white guy, maybe fifty, and he's talking to himself, and then he starts shouting, over and over, like he's giving a sermon, somebody's got to stand up for the character of the girls.

Ernest was really amused by that. He repeated it. People repeat what they like.

—Somebody's got to stand up for the character of the girls.

Two Greek women are in a field. One of them pulls an enormous carrot out of the ground. She says to the other woman, This reminds me of my husband. The other woman looks at the huge carrot. What, because of the length? No, she says. What, the circumference? she asks. No, the woman says, the dirt.

Elizabeth wanted a quiet night and a relatively good super. People got a little of what they wanted. No one ever got enough.

Across the street Frankie was closing the laundromat, pulling down the great, tired, yawning gate. Ernest and Elizabeth finished the last of the beer.

—I hate calling the cops, she said.

—I hate calling the City. Same difference, he said.

It was past midnight when Elizabeth said good-night to Ernest. Roy was in bed, and she lay down next to him. They watched the end of a "Honeymooners" episode.

"One of these days, Alice, one of these days, POW, right in the kisser."

Ralph Kramden threatened Alice, he never hit her. The morons were carousing in the background.

—Hector's been fired. We don't have a super, Elizabeth said.

—We never had a super. I'm going to sleep.

—You are? How can you?

—Easy.

She hated him now.

Elizabeth went to the window. Fatboy trotted over jauntily and stuck his nose through the gate. Elizabeth opened the police-approved window-gate doors, which she'd spent some real money on when they moved in, to prevent break-ins by spidery fifth-story men and to allow her, Roy, and Fatboy to get out fast in case of a fire. She raised the window as high as it would go, then the two of them climbed through and settled on the fire escape. Fatboy was happy. She wished she were him.

The morons were vocalizing, inventing their own brand of superrepellent sounds. Their whole existence was flawed.

Two Polish-Americans go to Poland, to see their ancestral home-land. They sight-see all day and at night go to a bar. One of them says to the other, I think that's the Pope. He points to a man at the end of the bar. The friend says, What would the Pope be do-ing here? I don't know. He could be visiting Poland like us, says the first. He's Polish. He could have come home, making a visit. I really think that's him. You're crazy, says the second. I'm going to ask him, the first one says. So he goes to the far end of the bar, and asks the man, Are you the Pope? The man looks at him and says, Fuck off. He walks back to his friend and tells him, I asked him if he was the Pope and he said, Fuck off. The friend says, So, I guess we'll never know.

Two of the morons rolled on the sidewalk, holding their sides, shitting themselves with goofy laughter. Three other morons and one veteran crustie looked on, bored.

There is no super. I'll murder them, one by one, she thought.

The worst person, John Wayne Gacy, who painted clowns and performed sadistic tricks in a clown costume for children in hospitals, then buried thirty-six boys in a tunnel in his basement, or Jeffrey Dahmer, who dissected road-kills when he was a kid, then turned into a cannibal who ate boys because he wanted to keep them from leaving, or the woman who dropped her infant out the window, or the woman who thought her child was possessed by the devil, so she scalded her to death, cleansing her of evil, the worst person is understandable, only human. Some people's wounds never heal. Cats let sick kittens die or kill them. The game was long over. The street jumpstarted and buzzed with an overflow of Knicks' victory high. Someone might get lucky.

A couple of the crusties on the church steps roused themselves from their stupor. They started hopping, whooping, and yipping. Elizabeth focused on the loudest moron. He was shrieking, throwing his fat head back and shrieking. She didn't think they could see her. Suddenly the loudest moron glared defiantly at the windows of people trying to sleep and turned his boombox up, as loud as it would go. He blasted it. It was an act of civil war.

Elizabeth lay down on the fire escape and went rigid. She kept her head low, her body flat, held herself back, and just stayed down.

Drop dead. Stop it. Drop dead. Stop it. Drop dead, stupid. Doing nothing was her civil right, doing nothing was her civic duty. Nothing is hard to do.

When Westley Dodd was little, he used to sit at his window and stare at the kids in the playground across the street. Dodd began exposing himself at thirteen, then he molested one hundred little boys, then he murdered three, took pictures of them. He confessed everything. He'd never been praised, he'd never been touched, he lived in an emotional desert, an emptiness, no one laid a hand on him for love or hate, and growing up as he watched the kids squealing in the school playground, all he could think about was how he wanted to hurt them. When he was arrested, he said he'd hoped to kill many more boys. He said he didn't think he had any feelings abour anything.

Elizabeth didn't have the right profile to be a serial killer, she didn't have a child to drop out a window, she had a lot of feelings, all her feelings were bad now, she had nothing against Fatboy.

One of the morons leaped on a car and banged it with a quart bottle of beer. The bottle shattered and several windows across the street squealed open. The ancient black woman with a Chihuahua came to her window, she was wheelchairbound, but she had a portable phone. She'd call the cops. They'd get right on it, they'd say, then they'd put the phone down and grin contemptuously at each other in the station house.

Last week an alarm pulsed and throbbed across the street on the top floor of the ancient black woman's building. A thousand-watt bulb blazed and flashed on and off, while the alarm throbbed and sobbed. Elizabeth phoned.

—There's something weird going on across the street.

—Yeah, we've had calls, we'll send a car. We'll get right on it.

For another hour the light flashed and the alarm whined.

Elizabeth phoned again.

—Did you send a car?

—Yeah, we sent a car. We didn't see nothing.

—The alarm's still going, and the light's still flashing.

—We drove past and we didn't see nothing.

—Did you look up?

They didn't look up. They didn't get out of the car. An apartment had been robbed and ransacked, the tenants were away, their alarm went off, the cops didn't hear it or see it, they didn't look up. They shouldn't be cops.

A man's disgusted. He just wants out. So he decides to go to a local monastery. The head monk says he can enter, except he must agree to take a vow of silence. No one in the monastery is allowed to speak at all, except for two words on New Year's Day. The man says fine. So he enters, and at the end of his first year, on New Year's Day, the monk asks him if he has two words he wants to say. The man says, Fruit stinks. Then another year passes, and the monk asks the man if he has two words he wants to say. The man says, Bed hard. After the third year, on New Year's Day, the monk asks the man, Do you have two words you want to say? The man says, I quit. The monk says, I'm not surprised. All you've done since you got here is complain.

A moron bellowed. A crustie turned the volume up on her boombox. Now two were going full blast.

Elizabeth climbed through the window, back into the apartment, and walked to the refrigerator. She took out a full carton of eggs and carried it to the window.

Roy opened his eyes when she was nearly out the window.

—What are you doing?

—Nothing.

—Don't do it.

—Don't worry.

She assumed her position and cradled a white egg in her hands.

The man in the third-floor window watched Elizabeth. She was strange tonight, going in and out of the window. He usually turned off his light before he started watching her, the street. He didn't think she knew he was there generally. Tonight she didn't look like she cared. He didn't know her name. Everyone on the block knew who she was because she was friendly. She was the kind of woman who sometimes didn't close her blinds. Not that she walked around naked. She wasn't a whore. She lived with a man. He saw the same guy there, not like some of the other women he watched, different men every night, the ten-dollar junkie whores on the block, like Jeanine, giving blow jobs in doorways, disgusting lowlife.

The man in the third-floor window imagined getting a blow job from Jeanine. He got hot, then he got angry. He pictured blowing her away, the disgusting bitch, her mouth to his joint.

A snail was crawling on a man's newspaper. The man flicked it off and the snail went flying. Five years later, the man's doorbell rang. He opened it, and the snail said, Hey, what was that all about?

The crusties were jubilant.

The fire escape hurt her ribs. Fatboy plopped himself on her ass. Elizabeth's view was straight down to the fire escape below, which had a few sorry plants on it and a wet package of Raid Ant Bait. Kills the Queen. Kills the colony. She could set a trap of silent-killer food on the church steps and see the morons eat it and die in agony.

In memoriam forget hope forget hopelessness forget innocence forget guilt forget lies forget truth forget good forget bad forget purity forget corruption forget vice forget virtue this is for you.

Elizabeth angled her head and body. She took a different position and looked around without moving. Her vision, peripheral and otherwise, was one of her best features. Elizabeth relaxed and released the white egg from her hand. A mild, humid breeze carried it. The egg cracked and splattered in the gutter.

Fatboy growled. The morons looked up. Elizabeth kept her head down, giggled, and whispered to Fatboy.

—Somebody's got to stand up for the character of the girls.

She extended her arm. She dropped another egg from a different side of the fire escape. It popped and cracked on the sidewalk. The yolk and white flowed, and the morons looked nervous. The loudest one looked up in her direction. He didn't see anything.

The man in the third-floor window was still, like a polluted pond.

The ancient black woman with the chihuahua was anxiously waiting for the cops. She took some notice of the white woman, but not much, it was just more craziness.

Elizabeth didn't care how she appeared to others. She saw herself.

Yes this is a fatal mistake or maybe just bad judgment it's no worse than fucking most of the guys I fucked no more stupid than trusting the people I have so it's really dumb and I'll be miserable it wasn't my choice I'm not that free I'll trade it all in the job the boyfriend the dog the friends the apartment and leave it all behind manacled and shackled by myself and I'll enter the land of the damned the spoiled and damaged race past everyone who's never risked anything stupid as this is they'll catch it later on TV people like disease and failure at a distance if they can watch it on TV it makes them feel safe especially when things are out of control everyone wants control things are going down there's no way to judge the speed of the fall no one admits the thrill the pleasure of giving up give it up give it up no one confesses to wanting to surrender be an untouchable who slinks along the streets a nobody who wallows in sublime degradation nobody's a dirty word yes I'm guilty take me away I want to leave the block I'm guilty OK.

When the cops arrived, the crusties would say someone was throwing eggs at them, that's why they were whooping, hollering, and blasting their boomboxes. They were just reacting, defending themselves against a sick creature sniping at them from an indeterminate fire escape, they were only battling an unseen enemy.

Elizabeth had an irresistible impulse to stand tall on the fire escape and address the block. She'd speak about the need for quiet. Abraham Lincoln spoke from the balcony of Cooper Union which wasn't far from where she was now. He delivered his second inaugural address after the Civil War ended: "With malice toward none; with charity for all."

One month later he was assassinated.

Elizabeth decided against standing up and being counted, she'd lie low and go uncounted. She wondered if statistically you were more likely to be murdered if you gave speeches. If you gave speeches in the wrong places, at the back of the bus, or acted inappropriately anywhere, you could be institutionalized, if you weren't already.

A Puerto Rican father comes home and doesn't see his daughter, but he finds her vibrator. The next night she comes home and finds him sitting at the kitchen table, drinking. Her vibrator is on the table opposite him. What're you doing? she asks. I'm having a drink with my son-in-law, he says.

Being appropriate was boring. She dropped two eggs together. The eggs, light as feathers, gathered speed as they went down. Gravity did its work flawlessly. The eggs hit hard on impact. They could hurt somebody. She hadn't thought about that before. Everything's a learning experience.

One of the crusties mooned the block. His ass was dirty, like his face.

Keep your big ass your big noise your big nose your big stink your big eyes your big lies keep your shit to yourself.

If the morons spotted where the eggs came from and spotted her dropping them, they'd be waiting for her tomorrow, like the plot of the scariest TV movie she'd ever seen, about a ten-year-old girl who sees a murder committed outside her school building. The little girl's dreaming out the window of her classroom and sees the murder in the distance, on a small hill, and the murderer suddenly looks in her direction after he's done it and sees her seeing him, and she knows he sees her, and she knows he'll be waiting for her after school, and she doesn't tell anyone. She's trapped in the school at three P.M. when everyone else goes home, and she's alone.

That was a long time ago . Elizabeth was eight. She turned off the TV before the end of the movie. Her mother had left her on her own and told Elizabeth she was her own baby-sitter.

It was pathetic. She was her own baby-sitter.

If the morons saw her, Elizabeth would alert the block. She wouldn't be like that little girl. She'd call Larry and Helen, she'd wake Roy, who'd probably tell her she was being stupid and to go back to sleep, and she'd fight the urge to kill him, which was inappropriate, she had to keep her attention on the real problems and enemies, and she'd alert Ernest, Herbert the deaf tenant, the acerbic super, Paulie, Gisela, Jeanine, and Frankie, and Ricardo, the whole neighborhood, she'd make up flyers, wheatpaste them on buildings, hand them out, she'd make it clear that she was being persecuted by the morons and crusties. She wouldn't be quiet, she wouldn't go quietly, she wouldn't fight alone.

Probably the young super would join the crusties and morons and take his stale revenge.

What were Kurt Cobain's last words?
Hole's gonna be big.

Elizabeth tossed another egg. It flew into the street, sailing on a bigger, wetter breeze. It cracked on the side of a passing car. The car slowed down a little then speeded up. Probably the driver saw the morons. Fatboy jumped up and barked. Elizabeth gagged him. She crouched beside him on the fire escape. She was wearing black, it wasn't planned, it was perfect.

She held her breath and her position, she was crouched and rounded like a basketball.

The ancient black woman phoned the cops again and stuck her body farther out the window. Elizabeth saw her speaking on the phone.

The ancient black woman would say:

—There's a crazy woman throwing eggs, and there are some unruly young people making noise. Please do something. I'm old, I live alone, I have a bad heart.

When the cops arrived, and they came to Elizabeth's door, and woke Roy, who'd be enraged, Elizabeth would say:

—The morons saw an egg or two drop over the side of my fire escape, by accident, and tomorrow they're going to come and get me.

The cop's eyes would narrow in contempt.

—Why'd you have eggs on the fire escape?

She'd have to go into it, her history, the story of the block, her night, her day, the last twenty-four hours, how she was driven to this act. She'd need backing from others, like Ernest. She'd have to mount a strong case, defend herself. Her heart was beating wildly, it was like a caged animal.

No I've never been in trouble with the law just a little I mean I never went to jail yes I lead a normal life I guess yes I've got a job part-time I had a few beers yes I've done coke grass speed no I told you I'm not high now I had a few beers yes I get along with people ask anyone in the neighborhood I don't have many enemies some I do I have some yes I like men I live with one what's that got to do with anything I don't think of those morons like that are you kidding no I hate needles I hate the blood and poking around in veins yes I have a temper I said I'm not on anything yes I vote what a question no I'm not married I was a little out of control I didn't murder anyone sure I thought about it wouldn't you no I'm not crazy maybe temporarily it was an impulse I couldn't stop no I don't believe in what I did it's not a matter of belief I just did it I'm not a member of anything a good life good sex is going to change this are you kidding are you guys going to keep them quiet every night I'm not a vigilante I didn't take any law into my own hands you must be kidding eggs yes I'm not saying it was right I don't care if it was right these morons don't care about anyone on the block they rob me of my sleep I'm robbed of my dreams no don't tell me about other people I'm not other people are we through now.

She'd explain that she corrected errors for a living, she came from a relatively stable family, there'd been more than enough food on the table, they had more than one table, they had a dining room, a den, a kitchen, a basement, and there were many tables, even a ping-pong table, she was a pretty good player. She'd admit that everyone bothered her eventually.

No one would protect her.

Rounded like a ball, her arms free, she could throw harder. She tossed another egg with energy. It catapulted from her and was lifted by a stronger summer breeze. The egg hit a parked car. The car alarm went off and screamed. It felt like her voice. One of the crusties clapped. Another crustie slapped him on the head. All the morons looked up in her direction. She was hidden in shadow. She'd made herself invisible.

A man died and went to Heaven. When he got there, he met God. He asked God, Please, before I go to Heaven, would you show me

Hell? I've always wanted to see Hell. God said, Yes, I'll show it to you. First of all, he said, Hell's divided into three tiers. And then God took the man to the first tier. It was a room with about eighty people. There was some wine and a violinist. Then God took the man to the second tier. It was a room with about three hundred people. There was a band and wine and some hors d'oeuvres. Then God took the man to the third tier. It was a large room with about eight hundred people, maybe a thousand. There was an orchestra, a band, champagne, and lots of food. The man was amazed and said to God, If this is Hell I can't wait to see Heaven. So God took the man to Heaven. It was a bare room with about twenty people. There was no food and no music. The man said to God, I can't believe it. This is Heaven? God says, For twenty people, I should hire an orchestra?

She tossed another egg.

This was her street, her club, it was a democratic party, an after-hours bar with beer in paper bags and morons on the sidewalk. The sideshow must go on. The moon was her night-light. Comic and tragic disruption was her nightlife. It was a joke.

She dropped the rest of the eggs, one after another. They cracked and splattered out of time like a lame chorus line. The acerbic super would go crazy when he saw broken eggs all over his sidewalk.

The morons threw themselves on each other and moshed in the street until a car came along. Then they split for the park. The cops arrived minutes later. They were useless.

There's no super. There's no one to complain to. There's everything to protest because she wanted everything, and she wanted more, and everything was wrong, and everything demonstrated, like a stupid protest march against herself, that she needed money, sex, respect, and her sleep, more of it all the time, so it meant she was getting old and cranky, and would die, because all good and bad things and people come to an end, and everything probably would before she did anything like buy a crossbow and arrow.

It made her sick.

The cops didn't see what the commotion was all about, there were no unruly kids on the church steps, they didn't see the eggs, they drove over some of them and crushed them into the street, they didn't look up, they didn't see her, they drove away.

The ancient black woman fed her Chihuahua and wheeled herself to bed.

The man in the third-floor window was frustrated. He couldn't go back to sleep. It didn't matter. It was Saturday. He didn't have to go to work.

Elizabeth hesitated. The street was dead. Then she climbed through the window into the apartment. Fatboy followed her obediently. She'd maintain a low profile, buy a white-noise machine, keep it next to the bed. Maybe nothing would happen. She slid next to Roy and poked him in his calf with her toenail. He was dead to the world, alive in another.

No one deserved to sleep. She wondered if she could. Elizabeth pulled the sheet over her head and waited.

# Acknowledgments

I'd like to thank C. Carr for encouraging me to do a book set in New York; Tom Keenan for our discussions, his enthusiasm and acuity; the MacDowell Colony for giving me a wonderful place to write, and all the people who contributed jokes: David Hofstra, Joe Wood, Paul Shapiro, Bob DiBellis, Eiliot Sharp, Mark Wethli, Jane Gillooly, Rick Lyon, James Welling, John Divola. Marc Ribot, Dennis Cooper, Larry Gross, Charlotte Carter, Andrea Blum, Osvaldo Golijov, Martha Wilson, Michael Smith, Dick Connette, Charles Karubian, and many others whose jokes have become mine. I'd like especially to thank Richard Kupchinsksas, Debbie Negron, and Ginette Schenk for talking with me for this project.

## About the Author

Lynne Tillman is a novelist, short story writer, and cultural critic. Her novels are *Haunted Houses*; *Motion Sickness*; *Cast in Doubt*; *No Lease on Life*, a finalist for the National Book Critics Circle Award; *American Genius, A Comedy*; and *Men and Apparitions*. Her nonfiction books include *The Velvet Years: Warhol's Factory 1965–1967*, with photographs by Stephen Shore; *Bookstore: The Life and Times of Jeannette Watson and Books & Co.*; and *What Would Lynne Tillman Do?*, a finalist for the National Book Critics Circle Award in Criticism. Her most recent short story collections are *Someday This Will Be Funny* and *The Complete Madame Realism*. She is the recipient of a Guggenheim Foundation Fellowship and an Andy Warhol/Creative Capital Arts Writing Fellowship. Tillman is Professor/Writer-in-Residence in the Department of English at The University of Albany and teaches at the School of Visual Arts' Art Criticism and Writing MFA Program in New York. She lives in Manhattan with bass player David Hofstra.

If you enjoyed *No Lease on Life* may we recommend other books by Lynne Tillman?

HAUNTED HOUSES

In uncompromising and fresh prose, Tillman tells the story of three very contemporary girls. Grace, Emily and Jane collide with friends, family, and culture under dark and comic circumstances, presented in uncanny, disturbing, and sometimes shocking terms. In Haunted Houses, Tillman wries of the past within the present, and of the inescapability of private memory and public history. A caustic account of how America makes and unmakes a young woman.

"In *Haunted Houses*, Lynne Tillman chronicles the loneliness of childhood and incipient womanhood, the salvation of friendship, and the neurotic chain that binds perpetually needy daughters to their perpetually self-absorbed parents. ... Her style is spare and compelling, the effect of clinical authenticity."
— *New York Times Book Review*

"Lynne Tillman's protagonists are so lifelike, engaging and accessible, one could overlook, though hardly remain unaffected by, the quality of her prose, with its unique balancing of character interrogation and headlong entertainment. Haunted Houses achieves that hardest of things: a fresh involvement of overheard life with the charisma of intelligent fiction. Its pleasures pull their weight."
— Dennis Cooper

"Ms. Tillman's characters are rigorously drawn , with a scrupulous regard for the truth of their inner lives…this is one of the most interesting works of fiction in recent times…Fans of both truth and fancy should find nourishment here."
— *LA Weekly*

"This complex and skillfully constructed novel has three separate storylines following the lives of three girls growing up in New York, maturing in a world of baffling freedoms and uncertainties.…Childhood fears, passionate friendships, sexual explorations, and the uncomfortable interdependency of parents and children are depicted with intelligence, honesty, and dark humor. But if you are looking for comfort and consolation, you must look elsewhere: Tillman writes about life as it is, not as we might wish it to be."
— *Sunday Times*

"Lynne Tillman's haunted houses are Freudian ones—the psyches of three girls, Emily, Jane, and Grace, each wrestling with the psychological 'ghosts' that shape them…Frequently shifting points of view are expressed in crisp sentences. Rather than forming a modernist stream of consciousness, however, the writing remains controlled."
— Lucy Atkins,*Times Literary Supplement*

"Lynne Tillman's writing uncovers hidden truths, reveals the unnamable, and leads us into her personal world of pain, pleasure, laughter, fear and confusion, with a clarity of style that is both remarkable and exhilarating. Honest. Simple. Deep. Authentic. Daring… To read her is, in a sense, to become alive, because she lives so thoroughly in her work. Lynne Tillman is, quite simply, one of the best writers alive today."
— John Zorn

While the tumultuous 1970s rock the world around them, a collection of aging expatriates linger in a quiet town on the island of Crete, where they have escaped their pasts and their present. Among them is Horace, a gay American writer who fears he has finally reached old age. Friends only frustrate him, and his youthful Greek lover provides little satisfaction. Idling his time away with alcohol and working on a novel that he will never finish, Horace feels closer than ever to his own sorry end.

That is, until a young, enigmatic American woman named Helen joins his crowd of outsiders. In Helen, Horace discovers someone brilliant, beautiful, and stubbornly mysterious—in short, she becomes his absolute obsession.

But as Horace knows, people have a way of preserving their secrets even as they try to forget them. Soon, Helen's past begins to follow her to Crete. A suicidal ex-lover appears without warning; whispers of her long-dead sister surface in local gossip; and signs of ancient Gypsy rituals come to the fore. Helen vanishes. Deep down, Horace knows that he must find her before he can find any peace within himself.

"Clever, witty, passionately written… Lynne Tillman writes with such elan, such spirited delight and comic intelligence that it is difficult to take anything but pleasure…"
— Douglas Glover, *Washington Post Book World*

"With *Cast in Doubt*, Lynne Tillman achieves several different kinds of miracles. She moves into the skin of a sixtyish male homosexual novelist so effortlessly that the reader immediately loses sight of the illusion and accepts the narrator as a real person. Alongside the narrator we move into the gossipy, enclosed world of English and American

artists and madmen living in Crete, and at every step, as the play of consciousness suggests, alerts, and alters, are made aware of a terrible chaos that seems only just out of sight. But what impresses me most about *Cast in Doubt* is the great and powerful subtlety with which it peers out of itself—Tillman's intelligence and sophistication have led her toward a quality I can only call grace. Like Stein, Ashbery, and James, this book could be read over and over, each time with deepening delight and appreciation."
   — Peter Straub

"Tingly, crisp, and wry. …Delightfully clever and probing."
   — Donna Seaman, *Booklist*

"Tillman's evocation of Horace and his life among ruins both geographic and aesthetic is a tour de force. *Cast in Doubt* recasts every genre it touches-the expatriate novel, the mystery, the novel of ideas-like a multiply haunted house of both form and identity."
   — *Voice Literary Supplement*, Best Books of 1992

"A private eye in the public sphere, [Tillman] refuses no assignment and distils the finest wit, intelligence and hard evidence from some of the world's most transient artifacts and allegories. This is a truly memorable book."
   — Andrew Ross

"If you can keep up with him, Horace will take you all kinds of places.… I was unwilling to close the cover and break the spell. I turned the book over and started over again."
   — *Boston Phoenix*

For the narrator of Motion Sickness, life is an unguided tour. Adrift in Europe, she improvises a life and a self. In London, she's befriended by an expatriate American Buddhist and her mysterious husband, or may or may not be stalking her. In Paris, she shacks up with Arlette, an art historian obsessed with Velazquez's painting "Las Meinas."

In Amsterdam, she teams up with a Belgian friend, who is studying prostitutes, and she tours Italy with deeply mismatched English brothers. And, as with an epic journey, the true trajectory is inwards, ever inwards, into her own dreams and desires…

"This is Jack Kerouac's *On the Road* rewritten by the opposite sex in the form of vignettes of far-flung places and implausible encounters … Impressions, associations, and bits of conversation jotted during lulls in a mostly manic itinerary, coalesce into a densely descriptive narrative. The result is a keen portrayal of the postmodern world&hellip."
—Ginger Danto, *Entertainment Weekly*

"Literature is a quirky thing and just when you start to believe it actually has been used up, along comes a writer, Lynne Tillman, whose work is so striking and original it transforms the way you see the world, the way you think about and interact with your surroundings…"
— *Los Angeles Reader*

"A close reading [of Tillman] yields just how much her characters do want to connect, while preserving the right to their own process of intellection, the life of the mind. *Haunted Houses, Motion Sickness* and *Absence Makes the Heart* are nothing if not testaments to the belief that presenting the quality of one's mind in public is a means of connecting to others beside the self. In scenes of degradation, annihilation or joy, she contends with the idea that one's thoughts and gestures, while seemingly at odds, are married…attempts to accept the other not as a mirror but as a self."

— Hilton Als, *Voice Literary Supplement*, Best Books of 1991

"A firsthand account of one woman's European journey and a riveting investigation of the troublesome notion of 'national identity,' *Motion Sickness* has true intellectual originality, a gorgeously sly dry irony, and a rich cast of thinkers and drinkers and eccentrics and hoods."

— Patrick McGrath

"An intense and personal narrative. People and events are approached obliquely and never fully explained, as if we might know them already. This lean book is a welcome change after the baroque excesses of much contemporary fiction. Recommended for sophisticated readers."

— *Library Journal*

The stories in *Some Day This Will Be Funny* marry memory to moment in a union of narrative form as immaculate and imperfect as the characters damned to act them out on page. Lynne Tillman presides over the ceremony; Clarence Thomas, Marvin Gaye, and Madame Realism mingle at the reception. Narrators—by turn infamous and nameless—shift within their own skin, struggling to unknot reminiscence from reality while scenes rush into warm focus, then cool, twist, and snap in the breeze of shifting thought. Epistle, quotation, and haiku bounce between lyrical passages of lucid beauty, echoing the scattered, cycling arpeggio of Tillman's preferred subject: the unsettled mind. Collectively, these stories own a conscience shaped by oaths made and broken; by the skeleton silence and secrets of family; by love's shifting chartreuse. They traffic in the quiet images of personal history, each one a flickering sacrament in danger of being swallowed up by the lust and desperation of their possessor: a fistful of parking tickets shoved in the glove compartment, a little black book hidden from a wife in a safe-deposit box, a planter stuffed with flowers to keep out the cooing mourning doves. They are stories fashioned with candor and animated by fits of wordplay and invention—stories that affirm Tillman's unshakable talent for wedding the patterns and rituals of thought with the blushing immediacy of existence, defying genre and defining experimental short fiction.

"Lynne Tillman has always been a hero of mine—not because I 'admire' her writing, (although I do, very, very much), but because I feel it. Imagine driving alone at night. You turn on the radio and hear a song that seems to say it all. That's how I feel…"
   — Jonathan Safran Foer